TAMING A WOLF PACK

I was halfway through a plate of pork chops and fried spuds when the five Hadley brothers walked through the doors of the Porter Cafe. Wilson and Carny made the command decision to seat themselves near the front of the restaurant. Their brothers filled up the table next to them.

"Say, sweetie," Wilson said in a gruff voice, grabbing Sarah Ann by the arm and pulling her down onto his lap.

"Let go of her, Wilson!" I said in a voice everyone could hear, even from where I sat. I was across the room in no time, determined to keep Wilson Hadley from doing any harm to my wife. I threw a cup of coffee into Carny's face before he could do anything. Then I grabbed Sarah Ann's arm and yanked her out of Wilson's lap the same time that I whacked the empty cup alongside his head. It wasn't as effective as laying a piece of deadwood up alongside him, but it had the desired effect.

I saw one of the other Hadleys go for his gun and was about to draw mine when Pa was standing in the doorway, his own Remington in hand.

"Boys," he said, "you even touch those pistols and I'll make sure you get a real nice burial tomorrow."

Books by Jim Miller

Shootout in Sendero
Stagecoach to Fort Dodge
The 600 Mile Stretch
Rangers Reunited
Too Many Drifters
Hell with the Hide Off
The Long Rope
Ranger's Revenge

Published by POCKET BOOKS

THE EX-RANGERS

8

SHOOTOUT IN SENDERO

JIM MILLER

POCKET BOOKS

New York   London   Toronto   Sydney   Tokyo   Singapore

An *Original* Publication of POCKET BOOKS

POCKET BOOKS, a division of Simon & Schuster Inc
1230 Avenue of the Americas, New York, NY 10020

ISBN: 978-1-5011-0949-2

First Pocket Books printing October 1992

10 9 8 7 6 5 4 3 2 1

Cover art by Garin Baker

Printed in the U.S.A.

*To Ethan Ellenberg,
for both saving my bacon
and supplying some of it.*

CHAPTER
★ 1 ★

You sure you don't want a drink, Wash?" my brother asked as we reined in our mounts in front of the Porter Cafe and dismounted.

I pulled my hat off my head and tried brushing some of the dust off my pants, but the more I got rid of the more I seemed to have underneath it. Chance and I had spent most of the morning breaking horses out at our spread, and had not been all that successful at it. It seemed like we had a particularly hardheaded bunch of mustangs to deal with today. I wasn't sure whether it was the weather or if these beasts were just downright mean spirited. Probably the weather, I'd told myself, for the nights were getting colder and the days weren't as warm as they had been a couple of months back.

"No thanks, Chance," I said. "You go ahead. I'm gonna stop in and see Sarah Ann for a mite. See if she'll rustle up a meal for me."

"Meet you in a couple of hours," he said before heading across the street to Ernie Johnson's Saloon.

"You bet." I knew good and well Chance was as much a creature of habit as I was. He'd spend half an hour drinking a beer or two, then make his way down to the Ferris House, the lone boardinghouse in Twin Rifles. Margaret Ferris ran it with her daughter, Rachel, who had taken a shine to Chance this past year or so. And the way my brother was looking at Rachel of late, why, I'd swear it wouldn't be long before the two of them would be tying the knot.

Me, I already was married. Only a year or so, but married to the best woman a man could have. Sarah Ann Porter had become Mrs. George Washington Carston nearly a year ago and I loved her with all my heart, knowing she felt the same about me. I reckon that was one of the reasons I hadn't noticed the cold nights as much as my brother, who had the room next to ours in our ranch house.

Sarah Ann was barely pushing twenty, but she was the prettiest woman I ever did see. She had golden blond hair and blue eyes that had the prettiest sparkle. And she was healthy as a horse, if you know what healthy in a woman is. But don't you ever tell Sarah Ann I said that about her. Vain as some of these women are, why, they'd shoot you upon hearing such a description.

Sarah Ann worked for her daddy, Big John Porter, who owned and operated the Porter Cafe. I heard Big

2

John say once that he thought Sarah Ann was one of the reasons his cafe constantly made a profit. Me, I used to think it was because the Porter Cafe was one of the only two places in town that served up a decent meal, the other one being the Ferris House. Of course, that was a good seven years ago, long before I even began paying that much attention to Sarah Ann.

"Hi, honey," Sarah Ann said in a chirpy manner, giving me a peck on the cheek as she left the kitchen and whirled past me, a tray of food held high in the air. In her other hand she carried a coffeepot. I smiled to myself as I watched her make her way to one of the tables and lay out the food. I always did like the wiggle in her walk.

"A look like that on your face, and you hadn't already married her, I'd make you," the booming sound of Big John Porter's voice said behind me.

"Oh. Yeah," I said, trying to turn a look of surprise into a smile as I took him in. If I liked seeing Sarah Ann walk, I liked it just as much when Big John had a smile on his face that accompanied his words. To say that the man was big would be an understatement. Let's just say he lived up to his nickname, which placed him a good seven inches taller than me, and I top six foot easy.

Big John gave me what I'm sure he thought of as a playful slap on the back as he said, "Don't worry, son. I used to look the same way at her mother." If there had been anyone sitting at the table I was sent flying into, I was sure I'd have upset them and their meal. "You look hungry, Wash. Have a seat over at that corner table and I'll fix you up a meal."

Rather than try to hold any further discussion, I did as the big man bade and took a seat at the indicated table. I'd no sooner set my hat down than Sarah Ann was there with a cup and the ever present coffeepot. I didn't have to worry about giving her my order, for both she and her daddy knew my taste in foods. I'd eat just about anything.

I was halfway through a plate of pork chops and fried spuds when the Hadley Brothers walked through the doors and looked as though they'd take up residence until they got fed. Half the time they'd bully you into paying for their meal and the other half of the time they'd order and then refuse to pay—at least until Big John showed up with that cleaver in his hand. They dug deep in their pockets then.

There were five of them and, just like a pack of wolves, they always traveled in bunches. But it was Wilson and Carny who were the oldest, the toughest and the meanest of the group. Chance and I had had run-ins with this bunch before, having grown up with them in this area. And as much as Chance and I had fought one another as younger brothers, I don't think we ever stuck together as much as when we were having it out with the Hadleys. Talk about going at it toe and heel . . .

Wilson and Carny made the command decision to seat themselves at the vacant chairs I'd stumbled into when Big John slapped me on the back. Their brothers filled up the table next to them.

"Say, sweetie," Wilson said in a gruff voice, grabbing Sarah Ann by the arm and pulling her down onto his lap. "How about fixing me up a—"

"Let go of her, Wilson!" I said in a voice everyone could hear, even from where I sat across the room. No sooner were the words out of my mouth than I was out

4

of my seat, the chair tumbling backward. To keep from pulling the Dance Brothers six-gun at my side, I grabbed hold of my coffee cup, which still held some of the hot liquid.

I was across the room in no time, determined to keep Wilson Hadley from doing any harm to Sarah Ann. Past experience told me that Carny would be right next to Wilson if it came to a fight, and suddenly I was glad I had that coffee cup in my hand. I was right at the table and threw the cup of coffee in Carny's face before he could do anything. Then I grabbed Sarah Ann's arm and yanked her out of Wilson's lap the same time that I whacked the empty cup alongside his head. It wasn't as effective as laying a piece of deadwood up alongside him, but it had the desired effect.

Sarah Ann was out of the way now, to my rear and safe, I was sure. But Wilson wasn't taking this lightly, not on your life. He was reaching down for his own six-gun when Big John suddenly appeared and grabbed Hadley's wrist in an effortless manner, pulling his hand up in front of him and slamming it down on the table. There was fire in his eyes and death in his voice as he looked at Wilson and growled, "Do you know how fast I can chop your fingers off, you silly sonofabitch!" That wasn't a threat that came out of Big John's mouth, mister. We're talking fact, and everyone in the cafe knew it.

I saw one of the other Hadleys go for his gun and was about to draw mine when Pa was standing in the doorway, his own Remington in hand. It was pointing right where it needed to be, at the three seated Hadleys.

"Boys, you even touch those pistols and I'll make

sure you get a real nice burial tomorrow," he said. He was all business too. The Hadleys froze in their seats like so much ice.

"You know, I'm gonna make me a sign to put above the door to my cafe," Big John said, addressing the Hadleys. "It's gonna say, No Jackasses Fed in This Cafe." To the customers in the cafe he said, "You folks see it, you'll know it pertains to the Hadley Brothers only. Jackasses," he muttered to himself as he headed back to the kitchen area.

"Good thing you stopped by, Pa," I said, a mite out of breath, although I hadn't really done all that much. "I was fixing to take on the lot of 'em by myself if I had to."

"Oh, I didn't really come to help you out, son," Pa said with a straight face. "Actually, I was looking for Joshua. I've got a prisoner for him to pick up."

CHAPTER

★ 2 ★

What you say the name of that town was again, Will?" Joshua squinted his eyes and gave Will Carston a puzzled look.

"Sendero, Joshua. Sendero."

"Now ain't that the blamedest moniker for a town you ever did hear?"

"We got our share of 'em, I reckon," Will said. "Hell, look at Twin Rifles. When me and old Abel Ferris decided to make a go of it, why, our rifles was all we had between us."

"Oh, I know, Will, I know. I've heard you tell that story so many times I likely know it by heart," Joshua said. "It's just that this one seems . . . well, it seems different, don't you know?"

7

"Not really," Will replied. "A *sendero* is one of those Spanish words for a trail, a path or a clearing of sorts. You stick around this Southwestern territory and you'll pick up a mite more language of the people who was here before us, I reckon." Joshua had been Will Carston's deputy since 1863, when he had shown up in Twin Rifles and decided to try the job on for size. Will was satisfied with his performance and Joshua had been wearing a deputy's badge ever since.

"Well, this place still sounds different, you ask me."

Will had finally found Joshua after the run-in with the Hadley Brothers. When he did he explained that there was a prisoner to pick up at a small, out-of-the-way town called Sendero. Or so the telegram said. The telegraph wires had come to Twin Rifles recently, leaving Joshua to wonder if he had much of a job at all. So in a way he felt a good deal of relief when Will told him he had an assignment for him, even if it was only to pick up a prisoner. Will had explained he would have gone himself were it not for the fact that he already had a jail full of prisoners, all of whom were being held on attempted bank robbery charges.

That was yesterday. Early this morning Joshua had packed to leave on his trip. His curiosity about the town of Sendero was the only thing stopping him now. But before he left, Will had made sure he told him that the prisoner was a part of the gang currently in jail for attempted bank robbery. The Richards Gang by name. Once back in Twin Rifles, he would stand trial just as much as the others for breaking that law.

Joshua had taken his time getting to Sendero, a two-day ride at the most. The days seemed cooler than they had been a month ago and the change in weather had been on his mind just as much as taking back a prisoner to Twin Rifles had been. When he arrived at Sendero, the first thing he did was take his horse to the livery stable and make sure he got a good rubdown and a decent feeding.

"I'll likely be back for him tomorrow, friend," he said before leaving the livery stable and heading for the saloon. He deserved at least one beer before finding a decent eatery, he thought.

For a small town, the saloon had as false a front as he'd ever remembered seeing on a building. Once inside, he'd politely asked for a beer and left a coin on the bar to pay for it.

"Quiet, ain't it?" he said after taking a sip of the beer.

"If you say so," was the bartender's reply.

"Come to pick up a prisoner," Joshua said when another sip was gone.

"Got papers on him, do you?" a man asked, bellying up to the bar next to Joshua. He wore the deputy marshal's badge of a city marshal. He also had a hard look about him, as though he were looking for trouble and had found it in Joshua.

"Why, of course I've got papers on him," the Twin Rifles deputy said and produced the official papers Will Carston had given him before leaving Twin Rifles. "Tain't like I don't know no better, don't you see?"

"Is that right?" The deputy lawman grabbed the papers from Joshua's hand and looked them over, shaking his head in disbelief once he'd read the documents. The next thing Joshua knew, he had a six-gun sticking in his belly, the deputy reaching across and relieving him of his own six-gun.

"See here now, just what in the devil do you think

you're a-doing?" Joshua asked, a certain anger filling his tone. But rather than try fighting the man before him, he unpinned his deputy U.S. marshal's badge and showed it to the man holding a gun on him. "I'm a federal lawman, don't you see? You don't put that pistol away, why, you're a-gonna find yourself in a heap of trouble."

But his words didn't seem to faze the lawman one bit. "Nope. You're the one who's in trouble, mister."

"Now, how can I be in trouble? Will you tell me?" Joshua said. "I just got into town and all I come for was to collect a prisoner to take back to Twin Rifles."

"That prisoner you come to collect? Well, he ain't among the living no more," the lawman said with a sneer.

"Well, how's that put me in trouble? Just what is it you're talking about, anyway?" Joshua asked, getting madder with each passing minute.

The lawman shrugged. "It's simple. We got a witness who says he saw the killer leaving the scene. And I'll be damned if you don't fit the description of the man he saw."

"Damn it, you let go of me or I'll—" Joshua said when the man grabbed him by the arm and tried to push him toward the batwing doors of the saloon. But he never did get a chance to finish saying his piece, for that was when the lawman brought his six-gun down on Joshua's head.

When he came to in jail, he felt an awful lot like he'd had the stuffing beat out of him.

CHAPTER

★ 3 ★

It was a good six days before I was able to take a breather from the horse breaking Chance and I do for a living and make it into town around noon for one of Sarah Ann's meals. Chance left for his usual beer and a meal at the Ferris House afterward. We agreed to meet back at the ranch to finish up the day's work later that afternoon.

If you were to ask Margaret and Rachel Ferris, they'd tell you that they were best of friends with Sarah Ann. And they likely are. I reckon about the only competition they have between them is the popularity of their foods. Sarah Ann has a recipe for fried chicken and deep-dish apple pie that I found hard to beat. And I'm not saying that just because she's my wife. Neither of the Ferris women would say so, but I had a sneaking suspicion that they would give their eyeteeth for either of those recipes.

Pa had already found a table and was sipping on his coffee and giving Sarah Ann his order when I took a seat at his table. "I've got a taste for fried chicken, darlin'," Pa said with a mischievous smile. "Why don't you give me a plate of that today."

"I'll have the same, honey," I said.

When Sarah Ann was gone, I said, "Joshua ever get back with that prisoner?"

A serious look came to Pa's face now as he replied, "No, and I don't mind telling you it's got me worried."

"Oh?"

"Sendero ain't but two days ride, and that's ary you're riding slow and taking in all the scenery," he said. "You know how Joshua is. Get it done and get it over with is the way he does things. He should have been back here a day or two back."

When he was silent, I asked the question I knew was on his mind. "You figure he's in some kind of trouble? Maybe the prisoner broke loose or something?"

"Or something."

The conversation sort of dried up then as Sarah Ann brought our plates of food and we settled down to do some serious eating. All a body has to do is remember the times he's been without in this land to take eating a hot meal real serious. And both me and Pa had done our share of doing without. It was only three years since the war was over, but both my brother and I could still remember those days when there weren't any rations at all, let alone cold rations to eat. No sir, I took a hot meal as anything but for granted.

"You don't think he could get in trouble in a place like Sendero, do you?" I asked, when I had just finished sopping up the last of the gravy on my plate.

"I don't know, Wash," Pa said, rubbing a calloused hand across his jaw in thought. "Time was I used to think a small town was nice and quiet. But since that war's been over, why, there's all sorts of riffraff passing through small towns. Just look at those yahoos I got locked up in my jail." Pa didn't have much respect for those who had taken up a line of work less than honorable these days. Especially the men who had come away from the War Between the States, having served for the North or the South making no difference. I couldn't say as I blamed him a whole lot either.

"You try wiring 'em back?"

Pa shook his head. "Just after this come in the operator said the lines went down. Claims it'll take him a couple of days to track it down and fix it."

"Want me to take a ride up that way and see what I can see?" I asked.

"What about all that horse breaking you and your brother been doing?"

I shrugged as though it didn't matter, and in a way it didn't. "Chance and me are about finished with the mustangs we last brought in. And Chance can go up to the draw to pick up a few more all by his lonesome. Besides," I added, "I could use the break. Get away from Chance and all."

"What about Sarah Ann? She can get awful worrisome when you leave town, you know." That was true enough, but once I explained what I was leaving town for, I was sure she'd understand. "And if there is trouble at Sendero, why, you're likely to be in a heap of danger to boot."

"You're forgetting, Pa, I was in the war for four years and come out of it in one piece. I hope you ain't gonna give me a hard time about being able to take care of myself." When I'd first come back from the war, Pa had given me a hard time about just that, all of which made me try the harder to prove my worth to him and anyone else who might question it.

"No, I reckon I've got no cause to," Pa said in a mite standoffish manner. "But you're married now, Wash, and you've got responsibility, what with Sarah Ann and all." I thought I saw my father gaze across the room at Sarah Ann in much the same way I'd seen him take in our mother's features so long ago. "It's just that—"

"Look, Pa, you've still got those prisoners in jail, haven't you? It's the same excuse you gave Joshua for not going yourself, remember?" I said, trying my damnedest to be convincing, knowing it could be right hard with Pa at times.

"Well—"

"Besides, his horse likely just threw a shoe or something like that. I'll leave at first light tomorrow."

"All right. But you've got to promise me to be careful, son," Pa said. I thought I noted a touch of worry in his voice.

"You bet, Pa. You bet."

I met Chance back at the ranch and we went over the ride I was going to make up to Sendero. We also made plans on things that needed to be done while I was gone, to include rounding up a few more mustangs. The army was always in need of fresh horses and we'd struck a deal with them to furnish as many to them as quickly as possible.

"This next bunch you bring in may be it for the winter, if weather gets any colder than last winter," I said.

"Yeah," Chance agreed. "We're gonna have to make our money stretch for three or four months, so this'll be the last bunch for quite some time."

I'd asked Sarah Ann to bring home any extra fried chicken she might have that night. As usual, it was past sundown when she did come through the door. Chance, who had been sitting on the porch, must have smelled the chicken as she drove up, for he volunteered to put the buckboard away for her in exchange for some. I gave Sarah Ann a kiss as she set the picnic basket of chicken on the kitchen table and wandered off to our room.

"You're going again, aren't you?" she said in a sad voice when she reappeared.

"Yeah," I said and explained that Joshua was overdue from Sendero and how Pa wanted me to go look into it for him. I wasn't about to tell her that I'd volunteered to go. I wanted to leave her on good grounds. "Don't worry, it'll only be for a couple of days," I said as I took her in my arms and held her close.

"But you know I'll miss you, Wash," she said in that soft voice she saved for times like this, times when she was talking to me and wanting her way.

"Chance will be here, so you've got nothing to worry about."

"But Chance won't be in town all day, like I will," she said, standing back and looking me square in the face. I thought I saw the beginning of tears well up in her eyes. From what she was saying, it didn't take much to figure out what she was getting at.

"Oh, don't worry about those Hadley boys," I said reassuringly. "It's just their nature to make trouble whenever they come to town. You tell Pa I said to keep an eye out for 'em and you'll be all right." I tried to wink and give her a smile, but I wasn't sure if it would work.

"Well . . . all right," she said after a while. "If it's only for a couple of days."

"Right. A couple of days." I only hoped she'd stay this chipper while I was gone.

CHAPTER
★ 4 ★

I had a notion it was going to be an early winter as I stoked the fire the next morning. Even with Sarah Ann in bed next to me, it had gotten awful cold the night before. Colder than I could ever recall it getting for the middle of November. I sloshed some water on my face, then filled the coffeepot with water in that gray light that comes before dawn. When I turned around, Sarah Ann was rushing into my arms, although with the bear hug she held me in, I was sure it was more than just the warmth of my body she was wanting.

"Morning," she said with a smile and a kiss. It was the same smile I'd seen on her face every morning since we'd been married upwards of a year ago. But I never did tire of it, and knew I never would. The woman was as fresh and new as the day before us. And if I ever needed a reason for living, Sarah Ann was it.

"Morning," I said in reply and gave her a playful swat on the butt, to which she let out a lively squeal.

In the next room I heard Chance roll out of bed. In a few seconds he appeared in the doorway in long johns and denims, a hamlike fist rubbing the sleep from his eyes. "You two have got to stop playing around like that in the morning," he said with as much a straight face as Chance could ever have.

"Why's that?" Sarah Ann asked with a curious smile.

"Listen, I know you two are trying to get me married off to Rachel Ferris," he said. "Trying to get me to give up my breakfast and rush on down to the Ferris House and propose to her, is what you're trying to do." He shook the cobwebs out of his head before adding, "Me, miss breakfast? Not on your life."

Chance was what Pa called a confirmed bachelor. "He likes the bait," Pa had said once when the subject of Chance getting married came up. "He'd just rather charm it off the hook than take a chance on getting caught." My brother had a firm belief in that line of thought too. As for missing breakfast, you could bet your last dollar that if there was food around at daybreak, why, Chance would find his way to it. But then I reckon he had a good excuse. He was several years older than me and an inch or two taller. He'd always claimed there was more of him to feed than there was me.

Sarah Ann set about fixing the morning meal for us while the ranch house warmed up a mite and Chance and I did some chores outside. Horses have to eat on a regular basis too, you know, and that was what we had the most of around here. Horses. Once we were back inside, Sarah Ann was finishing laying out plates of quickly prepared ham and eggs for us, just like she always did. I knew that she would then disappear into the bedroom to prepare for her workday at the Porter Cafe in town.

As I took a seat, Chance disappeared into his own bedroom and quickly reappeared, setting a leather covered oblong box between us on the table. "Want you to take this with you, little brother," he said, then fell silent and dug into the plate of food before him. Being in the war like we had, I reckon we both learned the value of a hot meal, especially on a cold day.

We sat there for all of ten minutes finishing off Sarah Ann's preparation before either of us spoke a word, and it was me who got the words out first. "Now, what in the hell is this?" I said as I poured us both more coffee.

Rather than open it up and show me, Chance first said, "Remember I was telling you how Kelly had been back East a few months ago? Some gun selling convention and all?"

I nodded in the affirmative. I knew it was going to be a cold day, so I was putting away as much warmth as my body could stand. I nearly drank half the cup of coffee in one swallow.

"Seems he met a fella named Thuer who works for Sam Colt's company," he continued. "Engineer, inventor, real handy fella, according to Kelly." The Kelly he spoke of was the owner of Kelly's Hardware in Twin Rifles. If you wanted a weapon and ammunition of sorts, Kelly's was about the only place in the area you could find them at in abundance. "This

Thuer fella, he applied for a patent for an invention concerning a metallic cartridge. You know, like the forty-fours Pa uses in that Henry Rifle of his."

"Yeah." Again I nodded. Chance was a fine story-teller. It was just that he sometimes took longer than usual to get the story out. I glanced past him out the window and saw the sun rising. "If this is a saga, Chance, you'd better make it a shortened version. I'm burning daylight."

"Sure. Well, Kelly talks to this Thuer fella and says he's interested in this invention of his. They go their different ways, but that ain't that."

"And?" I was getting edgy, wanting to leave right now.

Sarah Ann walked out, interrupting Chance's story. I thought I caught a hint of sadness in her eyes, although the smile she usually carried was still there. "I've got to go, honey," she said in her soft voice.

I walked her out to the buckboard that Chance had readied for her earlier and was now waiting in front of the ranch house. My brother sat there at the kitchen table, watching us through the open door, shaking his head in what I'd always thought to be disbelief, although at what I never was sure. Someday I'd ask him.

"You take care of yourself," she said as she left my arms and took a seat on the buckboard. She sniffled as she took the reins in her hands, was about to leave, then dropped them, reached over and grabbed me and pulled me to her. I wouldn't say it was the longest kiss I'd ever gotten from Sarah Ann, but it sure was the fiercest! "Damn it, you'd better make it back or I'll never speak to you again."

Then she was gone, the buckboard leaving nothing

but dust as she rode toward her daddy's place in Twin Rifles.

"Women," I heard Chance say behind me, in a tone close to disgust.

"Watch your mouth," I found myself saying in reply. I reckon I'd passed the point where I was no longer afraid of my brother and his size. And he knew it, for he was silent, at least on the subject of women. "Now spit out the rest of your story," I said as we walked back inside the ranch house. "I've got to git going."

"To make a long story short, it was just a week ago that Kelly got this package from the Colt Firearms people," Chance said, looking at the oblong box now before me. With the excitement of a young boy at Christmas, he opened it up. "Ever see anything like it before in your life?" I thought I caught a good deal of pride in his voice. On the other hand, Chance was proud of just about every weapon he'd ever touched or fired. If he had a specialty, weapons was it.

"What is it?" I didn't know exactly what it was, other than the fact that it looked an awful lot like my brother's 1860 Army Model Colt .44.

"It's a conversion model. It's what this Thuer was working on. An 1860 Army converted to use metallic shells."

"Is that right," I said with what I'm sure was a mite of awe to my words. I picked up the six-gun and carefully looked it over. It was the same size as the regular 1860 Army Model, but the cylinder had been reworked somehow. If I had any questions, Chance was quick to explain the weapon and its workings to me.

The percussion-cap cylinder had been cut off where

the nipples had been, refitted with a special back section with its own firing pin. The cylinder loaded from the front with tapering copper or brass self-exploding, center-fire, rimless cartridges by forcing them into place with the regular rammer. The bullet, Chance said, fit tight enough to allow the firing pin to explode the primer. In this Thuer Conversion, as he called it, the cylinder was made with the rear section containing the firing pin capable of turning separately on the center pin. A turn of one-sixth of a revolution of this breech brought an auxiliary pin under the hammer. When the hammer was snapped on this pin, the shell in the chamber on the right side of the one under the hammer was snapped forward by a blow on its base. Since the system didn't require any rebuilding of the revolver itself, the regular cap and ball cylinder could be used as before.

"I want you to take it with you," Chance said, pushing the weapon and its presentation box over toward me.

His words caught me off guard. I squinted at him as I said, "You sure about this? I thought you'd hoard every new pistol that came out on the market if you got the chance."

But Chance only shrugged in an embarrassed manner. "Hell, they'll have a hundred thousand of those on the market in a year or so. Besides, you're the one who's going on a mission, a mite dangerous one too, to hear Pa talk."

"You're sure about this? Honest?" I still couldn't believe my brother's words.

Again the embarrassed shrug. "I don't need a pistol to break a mustang. And that Dance Brothers piece of yours has an awful sloppy action to it." All of which was true. Like I say, if you want to know anything about the weapons on the frontier, just ask my brother.

"All right, I'll try it out." I hefted the weapon in my hand, pulled out the Dance Brothers six-gun I'd been carrying since the war started, and dropped the conversion model in my holster. It fit like it belonged there. I made sure to pack the Dance Brothers away in a saddlebag.

Chance helped me saddle up and get ready to leave. When I mounted up, I stuck my hand out to him and told him to take care of the ranch. It might not be like the bigger ones in Texas, but it was all we had.

"You take care of your own self, brother," he said, returning the shake with a firm grip.

"Listen, do me a favor," I said before riding off. "Keep an eye on Sarah Ann. I think she's worried about another run-in with those Hadley Brothers."

Chance grinned. "Don't worry. I'll keep 'em out of reach."

As I turned my horse to leave, it crossed my mind that in his own way, Chance was watching out for both Sarah Ann and me. After all, he'd handed over to me a brand-new six-gun, with a box of twenty-five of these new metallic cartridges.

"Watch your topknot!" I heard him yell as I rode off.

Without looking back, I raised my hand for him to see I'd heard him. I never did worry much about my topknot, truth to tell. It was usually my ass I had to keep from getting shot off.

CHAPTER
★ 5 ★

I knew Pa was a bit more curious than usual about what had happened to Joshua, but I also knew that it would be useless for me to ride clear to Sendero if the man wasn't indeed there. What if his prisoner had gotten away while he was returning and left him lying someplace for buzzards bait? What if his horse had thrown a shoe on the way to Sendero and he was just now arriving in town? Or leaving it? There were all sorts of possibilities, all sorts of things that might have happened. So I took my time and followed his trail as best I could, making sure it coincided with the directions Pa had given me.

He'd been gone for the better part of a week now, so most of the trail Joshua had taken was either washed out by recent rain or blown away by high winds. Still, I knew the general direction of the area in which this town called Sendero was located, so getting there wouldn't be the problem. Trying to find Joshua and what had happened to him was the problem. For the most part the tracking went well that first day, up until the end of the day.

I was heading down into the brush country by the end of the day. The Mexicans call it the Brasada country. It's just the opposite of that Llano Estacado piece of territory Chance and me drove Charlie Goodnight's cattle over, a barren piece of existence if ever there was one. The brush country is populated by a number of varieties of trees, enough that it makes you think you are in some kind of jungle area. At least, that's how I've heard it described. I've never been in a jungle of any type. Not unless you count some of that bayou land down in Louisiana and Arkansas, around the delta regions. Rather than rolling and flat plains, you'll find mesquite, post oaks, live oaks, Texas ebony, elm and pecan trees in massive growth. As thick as they can be at times, you'd think you were in a jungle. And I reckon after a good rainfall it likely seems that way.

The mesquites are as thick as the hair on a dog's back, and hoss, that's thick! Why, I recall Pa once telling us boys that they were so thick, he'd seen a rattlesnake backing out of 'em just to get away. I reckon they've been around ever since Christ was a corporal. Or forever, whichever comes first. Let's just say a long time is how long they've been here. The mesquite tree has bark that's thick and tough and roots that run deep to find water. I don't recall ever seeing one that was over thirty feet tall. That may be short when compared to those gigantic trees they've got in the true jungles of the world, but thirty feet surely does spread a whale of a lot of shade for a man riding through this territory. But it wasn't simply for the shade and a chance to make a fire for the night that I stopped under a grove of mesquites.

The mesquite produces seeds that grow in pods that look an awful lot like green beans. If you get them while they are green, they have a sweet flavor to them that is as sugary as cane itself. Pick them when the season is right and you can make a bean flour that is used to make tortillas. Fact is, the Spaniards had learned to mix it with cornmeal and make a right tasty flapjack of sorts. But this was late fall and most of them had likely fallen off the trees, which didn't bother me in the least. Much as I liked them, I didn't have the facilities or the time to go about making flapjacks. My basic concern at the moment was getting my horse some feed, and the mesquite beans I saw under those trees would make a right fine meal for my mount. You could find every kind of animal from deer to cows to horses and some in between that would feast on those beans. Even humans, Pa said.

I'd spent the whole day keeping an eye out for Joshua, or anyone else who might be in the area, and hadn't seen a single soul. Now, I'll admit that sometimes it seems like you spend your time sitting a saddle and don't get a damn thing done. Sort of like riding a rocking horse. Sort of like today. But I'll be damned if I didn't feel right tired for all I hadn't gotten done that day. And the farther the sun had gotten toward the west, the colder it had taken to be. By the time it set I was wishing Sarah Ann was there to share a blanket with me.

I found myself wondering just where Joshua Holly —that was his last name, you know—was laying his weary head tonight. But I didn't worry long, for the man could take care of himself, of that I was sure. Joshua hailed from somewhere in the mountain and Mississippi River country that separated Arkansas and Tennessee, if I recall correctly. His age put him somewhere between Chance and Pa, and he was as homespun as a country boy could be. For the most part he was easygoing, but I wouldn't go getting him riled for I'd seen him that way and he reminded me of a mean old grizzly coming out of hibernation when winter was only half through. No, there wasn't any use in worrying about Joshua tonight. Wherever he was, he'd take damn good care of himself.

I wasn't sure if I'd make Sendero the next day, even though Pa said it was no more than a day and a half ride, so I only ate half of the cold fried chicken Sarah Ann had packed for me. I hadn't eaten a noon meal, only stopped for some water and a cold biscuit, so I was hungrier than usual. I was working on the last cup of coffee when I saw my mount still having a good old time with those mesquite beans and figured I'd try some my own self. I picked up a handful, shucked the pod, and tossed them into my mouth and began to chew.

"Ow!" I all but yelled when one of them felt as though it had busted one of my teeth in half. I spit out everything in my mouth—beans, teeth, whatever it was in there that was rolling around loose—and took a gulp of coffee, somehow hoping the semihot liquid would ease the pain. It seemed to do the job and I felt less pain than I had a minute ago. I cast an eye about the ground to see if I had indeed spit out part of a tooth. At the same time I ran my tongue around the inside of my mouth and came to the decision that my teeth weren't any worse off than before. Except for that dulling sensation on the lower left side of my mouth. I spent the next half hour before turning in sipping what was left of my lukewarm coffee, which somehow decreased the pain I was feeling in my mouth.

My sleep that night was fitful at first. I'd almost fall off to sleep when I'd take a mouthful of that cold night air and back would come that pain in my tooth. I finally came to the conclusion that whatever was causing it, that tooth could stand only warm liquid or air. I wound up cutting a piece of cloth loose and folding it over a couple of times before stuffing it in the side of my mouth so it would cover the aching tooth. I could only hope I wouldn't gag on it sometime in the night and cause my own death. The thought was too gruesome to even speculate on what the tombstone would read if I died in such a manner, so I put it out of my mind and slept as best I could.

When I woke up it was colder than the south side of hell when the fire is out. I shook out my hat and boots before putting them on—no telling where some small animal might be looking for warmth in weather like this—stood up and took in a breath of fresh air, just like I always did.

It was a mistake.

I'd forgotten all about my bad tooth and, aside from nearly gagging on the soaking wet cloth I'd stuffed in my mouth, the ice-cold air had a horrifying effect on that tooth. I let out a yell, not caring who heard me as long as the gods of fate knew that I didn't like the way they were treating me.

I made it through breakfast and half a pot of hot coffee. By that time the tooth had settled down to nothing more than a dull throbbing sensation. When I saddled up to ride, I determined that the only way to keep the pain down was to keep my mouth shut.

I also wished I had Sarah Ann there with me. She knew how to handle things like this. As I proceeded to follow Joshua's trail, or what was left of it, I found myself remembering a question that stubborn young blond girl had asked me a time or two in the past.

"Why is it the only thing men know how to do is fight?" Sarah Ann had said in as mean a tone as she'd ever spoken to me. That was about the maddest I could ever remember her being.

CHAPTER

★ 6 ★

There was always a break between meals. It gave Sarah Ann time to help her father clean up after the last meal and to help in the preparation for the next meal. It also gave the two time to share confidences, much as they had always done over the years. But this morning things seemed different to Big John Porter. Especially in Sarah Ann and the way she was behaving.

"Careful now, Sarah Ann," he said to his daughter as he walked up behind her at the kitchen sink and placed a huge arm around her tiny shoulders. When she jumped at his touch, he could tell something was bothering her. "You keep rubbing those plates any harder and the shine will come right off of 'em."

When Sarah Ann looked up at him and saw him grinning from ear to ear, she knew he was only trying to fun her. Contrary to what some might think, John Porter had a very good sense of humor. She ought to know, for she had been experiencing it all of her life. It was just that the only time folks noticed him was when he got riled, for it was when he lost his temper that he was loudest and meanest and fiercest. She also knew that for a fact. Still, there were some things she despaired of telling him. That being the case now, all she could manage was a weak smile to the big man who had nearly brought her up by himself.

"I know, Papa." She tried to sound appreciative, but her words were just as weak as her smile. And Big John knew it.

He took the plate from her hand and set it down. Then, taking his daughter in his arms, he gave her a fatherly hug. He held her at arm's length from him and said, "Now, what is it, darlin'? What's bothering you?" When she said nothing, only offered a sad look that told more than she realized, Big John said, "Come on, Sarah Ann, you know I can't have a waitress who's liable to break down and cry right in the middle of carrying an order out to a customer. Why, you'll have food and dishes flying every which way," he said in a stern voice. "Not that the food ain't expensive, you understand. It's just that it takes the longest time to get new dishes from St. Louis, you know." He still had that businessman's look about him, stern as could be, but she knew that he was again trying to make light of a serious situation. "Come on, now, don't hold out on me. You've been my daughter too long for that to happen."

"I guess it's just Wash being gone and all," she said

31

after a moment's silence. "And trouble," she added cautiously, a shameful look crossing her face as she spoke.

"Oh, those Hadley Brothers, huh?"

"Papa, I really don't like it when those brutes paw me like they do. It makes me feel—" she started to say, but could do nothing more than shudder at the thought of one of the Hadley's mauling her like some wild grizzly bear.

"Oh, I wouldn't worry about 'em," Big John said in his most confident manner. With a wink, he added, "They spend most of their time outside of town, anyway. Besides, if Wash ain't here, I'll always be here to keep 'em from taking after you." When his words didn't seem to do much good, he scratched his jaw in thought for a moment, then said, "Tell you what, darlin', if you're really afraid they'll walk in any old time, here's what you do."

And Big John Porter told his frightened young daughter how to take care of bullies like the Hadley Brothers. When it got time to serve the lunch crowd, Big John thought Sarah Ann had shaken the fear that seemed to have taken hold of her this morning. Yes sir, he thought to himself, looks a whole lot more confident.

"How do, Miss Sarah Ann," Emmett said, one of the first of the noon crowd to enter the Porter Cafe. An ex-cavalry sergeant, he was a friend of the Carston family, often helping out Chance and Wash when they broke their horses for the army. He'd been known simply as Emmett ever since first coming to Twin Rifles, a year or two back. It wasn't often that he got into town anymore, tending to a ranch and family of his own outside of town. He took a seat and placed his hat on one of the chairs at his table. "Gotta pick up some ammunition over to Kelly's Hardware, so I figured I'd sample your menu."

"It has been a while," Sarah Ann said with a smile. She had always done her best to make her customers feel welcome in her father's establishment. "What's Greta been feeding you of late?"

"Mostly chicken," Emmett said in a puzzled tone. "You think maybe she's buttering me up for some occasion I done forgot about?"

"Thanksgiving's right around the corner, you know."

Emmett snapped his fingers, immediately remembering the date. "By Godfrey, you're right, Sarah Ann." With a wide smile, he looked at her the way a loving uncle might take in a favored niece. "I always said Wash married the smartest one in the family."

Sarah Ann blushed. After regaining her composure, she smiled back at him and said, "How about if I have Daddy fix you up a panfried steak, some home fries, and biscuits."

"You've got yourself a done deal, missy," Emmett said, a satisfied look about him as she walked away. Then it crossed his mind that something looked awful strange about Sarah Ann today. Oh, well, likely just his memory failing him.

It was twenty minutes later that the Hadley Brothers entered the Porter Cafe, as full of themselves as they had ever been. They also took up residence at the same two tables they had sat at the last time they were here. Emmett had his eye on the kitchen door, his stomach growling now, telling him it was time to eat.

He was really looking forward to that steak, especially after all that chicken.

Sarah Ann had a large tray of food balanced on her left hand, a full coffeepot in her right hand when she came out of the kitchen. She didn't even see the Hadley Brothers when Wilson stood up and pushed a beefy fist up under her tray, upending the entire contents on the floor. Sarah Ann stopped, standing stock-still, fear creeping back into her eyes as she looked at the big man before her.

Emmett was out of his chair in no time. "By God, that was my steak!" he yelled, quickly at Sarah Ann's side in no time.

"Shut up and mind your own business, farmer," Wilson Hadley growled. He was still staring at Sarah Ann, as though his looks could kill her.

"Farmer?" There was fire in Emmett's eyes as he spoke. He'd been called more names than he cared to remember during the war. But even out here he'd never been called a farmer. What the hell good were farmers? This was horse country. "You sorry sonofabitch," he added, as he hit Wilson Hadley with a hard roundhouse punch that knocked him back into the chair he'd gotten out of.

When Wilson tried to get back up, Emmett realized what it was that had looked so strange about Sarah Ann. She'd been carrying that damned coffeepot everywhere she went, that's what it was. And he found out why she did when Wilson tried to stand up and Sarah Ann tossed the entire contents of the hot pot of liquid onto his elsewheres. Wilson Hadley let out a scream that could be heard in the next territory, Emmett was sure.

Carny Hadley was next to try getting up, but Emmett hit him a straight left in the face, followed by a hard right that put the man in his place.

"Step back, Miss Sarah," Emmett said. "You don't want to see this."

"Papa!" Sarah Ann yelled out, just as she had been instructed to do.

Chance was just leaving the saloon when he heard the crash over in the direction of the Porter Cafe. He was on his way to check on Sarah Ann, just like Wash had asked him to, when he heard the crash, followed by a sound he was sure could belong only to Wilson Hadley. He lengthened his stride across the street and was about to take a step up on the boardwalk when Wilson Hadley came flying out the entrance to the Porter Cafe. He bumped into an older woman carrying a sack of groceries. She, in turn, was pushed into Chance's arms.

"Whoa, now, Mrs. Banning," Chance said as he caught the woman. "Are you all right?"

"Good Lord, what's happened?" the stunned woman asked.

Looking down at an unconscious Wilson Hadley, who looked as though he had wet himself all over, Chance could only shake his head. To Mrs. Banning he said, "Better step aside, ma'am. I got a notion this is gonna get ugly right quick."

Carny Hadley was the next to depart the cafe under less than friendly circumstances, whirling about and careening off a post propping up the veranda ceiling covering the boardwalk. Before he could get his bearings, Chance grabbed him by the shirt front and hit him hard, causing the big man to sprawl in the middle of the street, flat on his back. When he propped himself up on his elbows to regain his footing, Chance was there again to hit him hard twice, knocking Carny Hadley just as unconscious as his older brother.

Back at the entrance to the Porter Cafe, Chance was entering the establishment when he saw a third Hadley brother with his hands around Emmett's neck, choking him. He hit this Hadley hard in the side, so the man went buckling to the floor, then grabbed him in a headlock and dragged him out onto the street with his brothers.

The second time he went back in the cafe, everything seemed to be in order. Not that the fight was finished, for it wasn't. Emmett had a fourth Hadley pinned against the wall and was beating the living daylights out of him. What worried Chance most at the moment was the sight of Big John Porter. The cafe owner was sitting atop the fifth Hadley Brother and slowly but surely beating him to death with the flat side of his meat cleaver.

"Don't, John!" Chance yelled so the man would hear him. At the same time he grabbed hold of the cleaver and yanked it from Big John's hand. John Porter had a madness in his eyes Chance hadn't see in some time when he turned to see who had taken his meat cleaver. "You don't want to go to jail for killing some scum like that."

"But he attacked my daughter!" Big John yelled at him. Chance could tell the man was begging to have the weapon returned to him so he could finish the job he'd just started.

"Then I'll take care of him." The words came from

Will Carston who now stood in the doorway to the Porter Cafe, six-gun in hand, ready to handle anything. "Now, what seems to be the problem?"

"They come in a-looking for trouble, Will," Emmett said, dropping the prostrate body of the Hadley he had been beating, watching the body fall lifelessly to the floor. "That's the long and short of it."

"That's right, marshal," Sarah Ann agreed. Normally, she would call Will Carston, now her father-in-law, Papa Will, but this didn't seem like an occasion for anything less than formality. "I don't know about Papa, marshal, but I'd just as soon they stayed out of our cafe."

"That won't be hard to enforce at all, Sarah Ann," Will said. He then proceeded to grab one Hadley, then the other by the shirt collar and drag them out of the cafe.

"Thanks for helping out, Mr. Emmett, Chance," Sarah Ann said in a grateful voice. "I appreciate it."

"Hell, that was my steak he tossed on the floor," Emmett said, still a mite out of breath. "Do you know how long I've waited for a good piece of meat?"

"I'll put another one on the fire right away, Emmett," Big John said with a smile.

Sarah Ann accompanied Chance to the door. "I was just checking on you, like Wash said to do. Just in time too, it appears."

"So it would seem."

Mrs. Banning was shaking her head in disbelief as she watched Will Carston round up the Hadley Brothers and head them for their horses and a short ride out of town.

"Can't men do anything but fight?" the older woman said in disgust as she made her way down the boardwalk.

Sarah Ann had a playful smile on her face as she looked at Chance and said, "I've been saying the same thing myself for years."

"So it would seem," Chance said before walking off. Women. They were nothing but a puzzle.

CHAPTER
★ 7 ★

Pa was right about the ride to Sendero being a day and a half at best. I came on the town not far before the noon hour. And I don't mind telling you that what with the pain in my tooth, I was right glad to see the town in my sights. The trouble was, I still hadn't come on Joshua or the prisoner he was supposed to have picked up. If he actually had come to Sendero and picked up that prisoner, he must have taken a whole different route to get back to Twin Rifles for I hadn't seen hide nor hair of either of them so far. Not finding Joshua when I should have a long time back, why, that was bothering me something fierce, even more than my tooth.

When Pa had said Sendero was a small town, he

wasn't joshing. Not by a long sight. Judging by the size of it, I'd say it couldn't have had more than a hundred, maybe a hundred and fifty people on the outside.

There didn't seem to be but one livery stable in town either, and I pulled up in front of it as I approached town. An old-timer appeared at the entrance to the livery barn, a pitchfork in his hands. He gave me a dirty scowl, as though I'd disrupted his hay throwing by appearing in front of his establishment.

"And a good morning to you too, sir," I said, trying to get the words out all in one breath. Not that I'd gotten used to breathing through my nose, you understand. It was just that no matter how clumsy it might have seemed, it was far preferable to the pain the morning cold air had on my tooth.

"What the hell do you want?" he growled. When I was a youngster, I could remember Pa and some of the old mountain men he'd traveled with in his earlier days. Some of them were nothing more than pure relics of the Shinin' Mountains they'd worked in for twenty or thirty years. And those that had survived always seemed to have a crusty edge to them when it came to describing their personality. This fellow made them look like Saint Nicholas around Christmastime.

"Figured I'd give you some business," I replied in a calm voice, even though the pain in my mouth was killing me. "Unless, of course, you put up horses for free," I said with a leer. Sometimes I take on some of my brother's characteristics, which I don't particularly care for. On the other hand, this wasn't the most pleasant fellow in town—of that I was sure—and the pain in my tooth was getting worse with each passing minute.

"Two bits a day," he grumbled, still looking like the grouchiest grizzly bear I ever did see. "Extry if you want a good rubdown and feeding twice a day."

I dismounted, untied my saddlebags, pulled out my Colt Revolving Rifle from its scabbard and dug some coins out of my shirt pocket. I plunked a dollar in his hand and said, "This ought to hold my mount for a day or two."

His hand grasped hold of the coin as though he'd never seen one before. The furrow in his brow seemed to deepen as he looked at me and said, "Don't like smart alecks."

I shrugged. "I don't like ill-tempered old men who act like they've got a grudge to settle." I made sure I was looking him square in the eye when I said the words. "I reckon that makes us even."

The expression on his face didn't change one bit. Instead he simply grunted something unintelligible that I let pass as not being worth it. Besides, that tooth was getting more and more painful.

"You folks got anything close to a dentist in these parts?" I asked, taking in the main street of Sendero. There were only two saloons in town, one in the middle and one at the far edge of town from what I could see. The usual general store and mercantile buildings were peppered here and there. Also at the far end of town appeared a building that could only be a city hall or a building that would do for a church until the local circuit rider could persuade the townsfolk to build a more substantial one.

"Across the street, about two doors this side of the saloon," he said, his arm shooting out in front of him. The scowl on his face was still there, but I figured this was about as close to conversant as the man would ever want to become. I said thanks and headed for the building he'd pointed out.

FINNIGAN BROTHERS, the sign on the front window said in big bold lettering. In smaller print, underneath, were the words *Doctors of Medicine and Dentistry*. Upon entering the establishment, it looked like a one-man operation, that one man sitting lazily in what looked like a barber's chair, reading a yellowed-at-the-edges newspaper. Most of his hair was gone and his potbelly hung out over his belt, if he was wearing a belt. For obvious reasons, I couldn't tell.

"Sign says you can pull teeth," I said, setting down the saddlebags and rifle. "I got one that needs taking care of real bad."

"Well, let's see what you got, mister," the potbellied man said and climbed out of the chair. I felt myself get real squeamish about any ability he might have had to pull teeth when he smiled, showing a whole side of his mouth toothless. "Take a seat and let's have a look at you."

"You the dentist, are you?" I wasn't taking a seat anywhere until I knew that one piece of information for sure.

"Yep, that's me." Again the smile, again the toothless side of his mouth.

I took the seat, loosening the new Colt Conversion Chance had given me upon leaving home. I wanted this fellow to know that I wasn't going to stand for any shenanigans, not with my tooth hurting the way it was.

"I understand there's a prisoner in your jail here," I said before he stuck his fingers in my mouth, nearly prying my jaw open with their pressure.

"That's a fact, mister," he said, ogling his way into

my mouth. Something told me he wasn't married, at least not with the buffalo breath he had. I'd known stronger men who had wilted at the smell of such an odor. "They's a prisoner over there right now."

That meant the possibility existed that Joshua might never have reached this town in the first place. If the prisoner was still here, he might have gotten bushwhacked on the trail up here, although I couldn't recall seeing any indication of such an incident taking place. Things were getting stranger and stranger in this town, I told myself.

He turned my head one way, then turned his own head another, the look on his face screwing up almost as bad as that old-timer at the livery stable.

Suddenly, I heard voices in the room next to us, two men arguing about something or other, neither one seeming all that satisfied with what the other said. Then the words stopped and the door to the back room swung open. Out charged a young man of eighteen or nineteen years of age. Even with his hat pushed down over his eyes, I could see that I had a few years on him. Even so, if the look about him was any indication I wouldn't want to tangle with him. Not right now, at least.

"You can go to hell, doc, for all I care," he said in a hard, even voice, followed by a fit of coughing. He spit out a large gob of something and hit the spittoon right where he'd wanted to. He stood still for a moment until the cough subsided then, giving the doctor he'd spoken to an ugly glare, he stormed out of the room, slamming the door as he left.

The doctor, if that was what he was, did nothing more than watch him go, shaking his head in disbelief. "That young man is in for some rough times if he doesn't take care of himself," he said as he watched the young hellion go.

"Got what you thought, does he, Abel?" my friend the dentist said, taking time out for conversation while he left his fingers in my mouth. I grabbed his hands and yanked them away from my mouth, nearly gagging on the spit that had been sitting in my mouth. I didn't hit the spittoon.

"I'm afraid so, Rufe," the doctor named Abel said. Then to me, as though not wanting to leave me out of the conversation, he said, "Consumption, you know. If he doesn't take care of himself—"

I turned to Rufe, the apparent dentist. "Mister, are you gonna pull my tooth or not?" If I sounded a mite angry it was because I was. Like I said, the tooth and all that.

"Hell, no, I'm not gonna pull your tooth!" Rufe said with a look about him as though I'd slapped his face. "Not with you keeping a hand on that six-gun you're a-packing. Hell, no!"

In a way I could understand his line of thought, for I did indeed have my hand over that Colt Conversion. And I had to admit that the way I was feeling, if this man hadn't taken out the right tool, why, I likely would have done serious harm to him with my pistol.

"Tell you what you do, mister," Rufe said in a speculative manner. "You go a couple of doors down to the saloon and have you a couple of drinks. Just make sure you swill that whiskey around in your mouth and on that tooth. Onliest way I can think of at the moment to bring the pain down. You tell old Jed the first two rounds is on me, all right?" he added with that toothless smile, giving me a slap on the back.

"You make it sound like I could spend the rest of my

life carrying around a bottle of Who-Hit-John," I said with a frown.

"Many's a friend has been made with John Barleycorn that way," was his reply. "Yes, sir." The temperance folks wouldn't stand a chance around this fellow, of that I was sure.

I turned to leave but old Rufe the dentist wasn't through with me yet.

"That'll be four bits," he said, hand held out before him, palm facing up.

"What for? You didn't pull my tooth." I had a notion the look on my face was now a lot like the old-timer down at the livery, for all the disappointment I was feeling.

"Time is money, friend," Rufe said with a grin. "Gotta pay the rent, you know." He still had his hand out for payment.

I frowned again as I dug inside my pocket one more time for more coins. Two drinks free? My eye and Betty Martin! I plopped the coins in his hand and was about to leave when a thought occurred to me. I stopped at the door and faced him.

"That prisoner. Do you know his name? What he's in jail for?" I asked.

"Don't know his name," Rufe said, pocketing his change. "But he's in there for murder, he is."

That didn't sound at all like the prisoner Pa had sent Joshua after. I wracked my mind as I left his office, sure that the man Joshua was to pick up was some sort of bank robber.

Like I said, this was getting to be a strange town.

CHAPTER

★ 8 ★

I never was much of a drinking man, although I'll admit to having a beer or two and maybe even a shot of whiskey now and again. If there was a man in our family who liked to drink, I reckon it was my brother, Chance. Next to eating and shooting off those guns of his, I reckon drinking a beer came in a close third for Chance. But today I was needing a drink real bad, so I headed for the saloon Rufe had pointed out to me. I was just hoping that swilling some red-eye around in my mouth was going to kill the pain like he was saying it would. For a dentist, he sure didn't seem too ambitious as far as making a dollar at his trade went.

The Avalon Saloon was no bigger or smaller than Ernie Johnson's back in Twin Rifles. Not at first glance, anyway. The false front and batwing doors were there, although it was cold enough for the larger doors behind the batwings to be closed now. The big plate glass window had fancy squiggles and such decorating it, just like Ernie's place. But I didn't stop to admire it where I once might have, for that tooth was getting more and more painful, especially out here in the cold wind.

A voice or two made sure to tell me to close the door no sooner than I had it open, but the frown I gave them shut them up and they went back to their beer, or whatever they were drinking.

"Whiskey," I mumbled out of the side of my mouth as I leaned on the bar and rubbed the side of my mouth. The bartender must have seen what my problem was, for he poured me a tumbler rather than the small shot glass reserved for most customers.

"With that kind of problem, I won't charge you more than regular price either," he said, with what he must have thought to be a sly grin.

"Thanks," I said and took a swallow of the dark colored liquid that sat before me. I swallowed half of it and swished the rest around in my mouth, leaving a good deal of it set on the infected tooth. What I swallowed made me feel warmer on the inside, which helped some. As for the tooth, well, some of the pain did indeed go away, although not all of it. Still, it was better than it had been.

"Had the darnedest toothache about a decade ago," the bartender said by way of reminiscence. I wasn't particularly keen on hearing any of his stories right now, but what could I do? After all, I had a mouth full of whiskey and he must have known what I was trying to do with it. Hell, he had me trapped. "Near wished I had me a hammer to bust my jaw open, it was that bad."

"Know what you mean," I said when I swallowed the rest of the whiskey. "Ouch!" I grimaced again as the pain came shooting back. Just because the whiskey had dulled the pain, I had thought I was on the road to recovery, but it was a big mistake. As soon as the air had come rushing into my mouth, the pain in the tooth had increased tenfold and I was feeling just as bad as when I'd walked in. "Damn it," I mumbled before taking another gulp from the tumbler and going through the same routine.

"Looks like you had as much luck with the dentist as I did with the doctor." At first I didn't recognize the voice, at least not as one I knew. Then I saw him moving down the bar, closer to me, and knew it was the young man I'd seen charging out of the dentist's office. As dark as the inside of the saloon was, I knew I wouldn't have to see him to know who he was. He coughed heavily and spit to the side as he moved toward me.

I nodded hello to him.

He wasn't especially big—stocky might have been more like it. I had a couple of inches on him in height but found myself feeling cautious about the man just the same. I've been around long enough to know that a man's size doesn't mean squat when it comes to toughness. He had brown hair and eyes and a face that could well be leathered by the effects of a few years of weathering winter storms and droughty summers. If I had to pick a word to describe him, I'd have to say feisty fit him well.

He had a half-empty bottle of whiskey before him which he'd pushed along the bar top as he neared me

"Name's Riley," he said and poured a generous amount of liquor into my near empty tumbler.

I swallowed the terrible tasting stuff in my mouth, nodded again, and said, "Wash Carston. Thanks for the whiskey." This time I took in less than a full gulp and did so before I could feel any pain coming back to the tooth. Damn, but this was getting to be a vicious pain I had in my mouth.

"Tooth, huh?"

I nodded.

"Hmm. Which one might it be?" he asked in a curious manner. At least he showed more concern than Rufe, who I had my doubts about as far as dentistry went.

I swallowed the whiskey, grit my teeth and bared them for this stranger who had taken a sudden interest in my well-being. I pulled down my lip with a finger and pointed to the fourth tooth back on my lower left jaw.

He took a gander, coughed and spit to one side, then simply shrugged. "Don't look all that bad."

"Ah, but you don't know how it *feels*," I said quickly with a mumble. I couldn't imagine speaking like this the rest of my life, sounding like some damn fool who couldn't get his words out right. I'd likely be known as the man with Tanglefoot of the Tongue.

"That's a fact," he said, nodding in agreement. Then he did something odd. He gave me a curious look, cocked an eye toward me, taking in my face it seemed. Then his line of sight shifted off to my right, somewhere back in the rear of the room. He frowned a mite, then turned to me and said, "Say, do you know that feller back there?" With his left hand he pointed where he'd been looking.

49

When I turned to look I felt confused for there was no one back where he had indicated. Then, just before it happened, I felt as though I'd walked into an ambush.

I turned to face him, which is when he hit me with a hard right, right across the jaw. He knocked me ass over teakettle, leaving me sprawled out on the floor and flat on my back. There was blood in my mouth. I leaned over and spit out a mouthful as I slowly got to my feet, ready to take on this yahoo toe and heel if that was what he wanted.

"Whoa, now, partner," he said, coughing as he held a hand up to me. "I ain't looking for no fight."

"Then what the hell did you hit me for!" My jaw hurt as I spoke the words, hurt almost as much as the tooth that had been giving me all that pain. "Damn near busted my jaw."

He spit out what he'd coughed up and bent down to the spot where I'd left a gob of blood on the floor. "Is that all that's hurting, your jaw?" he said as he bent down.

"Yeah, but damn it, that hurts," I said. Then suddenly, something felt strange about me. My jaw still hurt like hell, to be sure, but something was missing. I spit out another mouthful of blood.

"It worked then," Riley said, standing up straight and showing me a small white piece of something he held in his hand.

"Well, I'll be damned," I muttered to myself as I looked closer at his hand. Bigger than God made green apples, there was my tooth. It had to be my tooth, for that was what was missing. I swished my tongue around then dug a finger inside my mouth and found the rotten tooth gone, although the area was still a mite bloody. The pain in my tooth was gone now, replaced by the pain from this man hitting me on the jaw.

"Claude, I'm gonna borrow your spittoon," Riley said to the bartender. Then he grabbed a spittoon in one hand and took hold of my elbow with the other, leading me over to a vacant table, off to the side from the others. Before I could say anything, he had me in a seat and was saying, "Just take enough of that whiskey to swish around a minute or two and spit it out. You keep swallowing it like you was, why, you'll get sicker than my aunt Sarah."

I didn't know who his aunt Sarah was, but he was right about swallowing the whiskey. Any more of the stuff and I'd be losing what little food I had in my stomach.

"You hit awful hard, friend," I said after spitting out a stream of reddish liquid that was a combination of blood and whiskey.

"I generally hit what I aim at," he said with a hint of a smile. Like I said, he gave the impression of being a cocky young man.

"You didn't seem all that tough charging out of that doctor's office," I said, taking another sip of the whiskey and swishing it around in my mouth. If nothing else, I figured it would gather up all the loose blood in my mouth and any I might have left in the hole vacated by my tooth. It seemed to be doing the trick too.

The smile quickly vanished from his face, replaced by a sad frown. For a man who was real fast to take an interest in my affairs, he didn't seem like he wanted to discuss his own. Not that you could blame a fellow. If there's one thing I've learned over the years it's that dying never is a popular subject when it comes to speaking of it. Tends to remind a body of how mortal he really is, I reckon.

"Look, mister—"

"The doc said you had consumption," I said, interrupting him. I figured I'd save him the embarrassing need to tell me to mind my own business.

He coughed harshly, as though he were about to lose a lung over it, then gathered up a whole lot of spit in his mouth and sent a stream of it toward the spittoon. He hit his mark easily.

"What of it?"

"My pa says most men spend their time up in the Rockies or down around Old Taos when they want a cure for it," I said, trying my best to sound neighborly. "Heading that direction, are you?"

He was silent in his own thoughts for a while, me taking a few more swallows of whiskey and depositing them in the spittoon after they'd done their job. I found the less I moved my jaw, the better it was feeling. But that awful pain from my tooth was definitely gone, a fact which made me feel a whole lot better. A whole lot better.

Finally, in a somewhat somber voice, he said, "Had a tooth pulled sometime back." With a shake of his head, he smiled as though recalling the event. "Hurt worse than having a bullet taken out, I swear."

"You won't get no argument from me on that," I replied.

"I just figured I'd inflict less pain on you than that goddamned dentist would." I assumed he was referring to the whack on the jaw he'd just given me.

In a way what he said made sense. "In that case, I appreciate your help, Riley," I said, although I wasn't sure whether I was giving the man thanks or excusing him for what he had done. Maybe both. "I think."

"Any time." He went back to nursing his drink then, again silent in his own thoughts. Me, I couldn't help but wonder if it wasn't the consumption that was heavy on his mind. I know it sure would be on me if that was my condition. As I'd told Riley, Pa had mentioned some of his old saddle pards heading for the Rockies or Old Taos to treat the condition. Drier climate and all, you understand. But for the life of me, I couldn't recall him ever telling what happened to the men once they took the cure. For all I knew, they could all have died shortly after. It got me to feeling not only a bit curious about the young man whose table I shared, but maybe a mite sorry for him too.

"I know it ain't none of my business, friend, but did that doctor give you a time limit on this consumption and how long you'd have it?" I asked in what was likely a skittish manner. Saying the wrong thing in this land can get a man killed in some instances. Prying into a man's personal affairs . . . well, you can't find a surer way of asking for a fight in many a man.

Riley coughed and sputtered and spit before he was able to give me a hard frown that said yeah, he knew it was none of my business too. Then he said, "Aw, to hell with it. The old quack says six months if I'm lucky." The look and voice got harsher and meaner as he added, "That satisfy your curiosity?"

"Look, Riley, I didn't mean nothing by it," I said, holding my hand palm forward, just as he'd done to me earlier. "I was just wondering . . . well, whether there was anything I could do for you or not. I'm not a doctor or anything, you understand, but . . ."

Quietness came over him and he was studying his

whiskey glass more than my face. In a half-ashamed tone that was almost a whisper, he said, "No. No, there's nothing you can do for me, Carston. Not a damn thing." As soon as his words were out, a spasm of coughing hit him. I wondered how painful it must be for his lungs, all that coughing.

He finished off his drink, quickly pouring and downing another shot glass full of the brown liquid. It didn't take much to see he was wanting to be alone now, so I thought better of asking any more questions. The way he was drinking, I figured he only had one thing in mind and that was getting blind ass drunk. The trouble with that is you're also likely to start feeling sorry for yourself, and that's no good for anybody.

"You know, Riley, I'd hate to see you sitting there feeling like the world owes you a living," I said as I rose from my chair.

"And what's that got to do with the price of cotton?" he asked in a puzzled manner.

"Pa always said a man ought not to act like the world owed him a living because it was here first." So much for philosophy.

"I see." If he paid any attention to my words, he didn't indicate so. Instead he concentrated more on the amount of whiskey that was in the glass and bottle before him.

I turned to go, then stopped, figuring I'd take one last stab at trying to be a friend to this man.

"Riley?"

"Yeah?"

"Why don't you call me Wash? Most of my friends do."

He studied my face for a moment in silence, then said, "I'll keep that in mind."

"Thanks for helping out," I said, although I still wasn't sure what was meant by those common words in this instance.

"Anytime," was all he said as I left and he went back to work at killing that whiskey bottle.

CHAPTER

★ 9 ★

I knew I'd have to get something in my belly before long, but first I was going to check on what I'd come here for in the first place. I won't say that the whiskey cleared my mind any, but finally getting rid of that pain I was experiencing definitely made me feel better about getting things done.

I stood in front of the saloon, taking in the main street until I spotted the office of the local law. Even if the sign hadn't been hanging in front of the entrance, I'd still have been able to make it out. Usually, the marshal's office is about the only building in town that has bars across its front windows. So I found it in no time and made my way to the entrance. The wind was picking up some so I found myself taking longer than usual strides as I crossed the street.

The inside was as much like Pa's office as I'd figured it to be. A couple of cells side by side in the back of the room. The marshal's oversize desk was sitting square in the middle of the room. A rifle rack had been built into the far wall to my immediate right, and it was loaded for bear if the weapons hanging on it were any indication. And, just like Pa's office, there was the ever-present smell of coffee in the air.

"Fresh brewed?" I said right off as I entered the lawman's office.

The nameplate sitting on the desk said FORREST HANEY in big bold letters.

The man behind the desk had been going over some old wanted posters as I walked in on him. As soon as I spoke he was on his feet, making sure the city marshal's badge on his chest was in plain sight for me to see. He was tall and heavyset and at least twenty years my senior. Having been in the field of law enforcement for a good deal of my life—I'd spent my years before the war with Pa and my brother, Chance, in service as a Texas Ranger—I knew the lines on his face were like most of his breed. They were war maps, trails, and battles that few other men could boast of having partaken in. Men like this had been up the creek, over the mountain, down into the cave and back. They were men to be respected, and that was that. "That depends on who wants to know," he said, a cautious frown about him.

"Wash Carston, from up Twin Rifles way." I took off my hat and brushed it against the side of my pants. Call it a sign of respect, if you will. On the other hand, a hat can hide a lot of a man's features, and I wanted this man to see who I was without a doubt.

"Help yourself, Carston," he said after giving me a going-over. I reckon I wasn't on any of his wanted posters. "Pull up a chair."

I stood by the potbellied stove warming myself before I poured some coffee. As I did, I explained that I'd been sent down to pick up a prisoner.

"A prisoner?" he said in a puzzled tone. There seemed to be a lot of puzzlement going around in this town. "I don't have a prisoner for Twin Rifles. Oh, I did a few days back but he's no longer here."

"He get picked up by another lawman, did he?" I asked. Now I was the one who found himself being cautious, for this wasn't what I'd been expecting. It wasn't what I was looking for.

"As a matter of fact, he got shot while trying to escape, son." There was another moment of pause before he added, "The only prisoner I've got is the one over there sleeping." He pointed to a man lying down in one of the cells.

"Who is he?"

"I'd appreciate it if you'd stay away from him," the marshal said as I started to rise from my seat. "He's an awful mean type. Got him in for murder."

All the time he was talking I was staring at the lone figure on the cot in the cell. I squinted, then frowned, then squinted some more. There was something awful familiar about that man. Ignoring the lawman's request, I got up and walked over to the cell.

"Joshua?" I said in astonishment.

The body stirred and the hat fell to the side of the man's head as he awoke and rolled to a sitting position.

"Wash? Is that you?" he said in just as much awe as there had been in my own voice. No wonder I couldn't find any sign of him returning to Twin Rifles. He'd never left Sendero!

"What the hell are you doing here?" I asked.

"Like I said, he's in for murder." The marshal sounded firm in his convictions and somehow I knew he wouldn't budge from that stance. "Now you get away from that cell." Before he was finished speaking, he had an iron grip on my arm and was guiding me back to the seat at his desk. I've got to tell you, hoss, I was starting to get tired of people leading me around by the arm. I couldn't remember that being done to me since back when I was a youngster and living at home.

"It's a long story, Wash, and you ain't a-gonna believe it when you hear it," Joshua said as the lawman was dragging me away from his cell. While I was being seated, I noticed for the first time that Joshua was looking a mite on the haggard side. He had a bruise on one cheek and the telltale marks of a black eye over his left eye. The hair on the side of his head was caked with dried blood and looked as though it were just now healing. Joshua hadn't fared too well in his stay here.

"You've got to let him go, marshal," I said in a determined voice of my own as I adjusted myself in my seat and the marshal took back his own.

"Son, I don't *got* to do nothing, especially if you say so," he growled. He seemed a little less than impressed with my attitude, but then you don't let a friend down without a fight. That's just not the way I was brought up to believe about friendships. True, I hadn't known Joshua any longer than I'd been home from the war, but that had been a few years now and I'd found him to be as good a deputy as Pa could ever want or need. We all knew that Joshua could be cantankerous as all get out, but we also knew that he had a good sense of humor too, and in this land that helped a lot at times.

It was then I remembered what I should have done in the first place and that was produce a badge for this man to see. I should have unbuttoned my coat and let him see it from the start, but I'd been so damned cold that I'd clean forgotten about it. I did so now and pulled back the coat, letting him see the deputy U.S. marshal's badge I wore. Pa had sworn me in as one, which in theory gave me the powers that go along with the badge.

Forrest Haney wasn't impressed.

"I hope you ain't gonna try pulling your weight around, son," he said, a half sneer filling his face, "because it ain't gonna work with me. I've had some of the best try and buffalo me and it just don't work."

"Will Carston's the federal man in Twin Rifles, marshal, and he sent me to look for this man," I said, indicating Joshua. "I've found him, and now I'm gonna take charge of him. You want him here for a murder trial, you let us know and he'll be here."

"Got papers on him, do you?"

"No, but—"

"Study up on your law, son, especially if you're gonna wear a federal man's badge," he said, his voice getting a mite harder now. "You want to transfer him out of my jail, you'd better have you some papers that say I've got to turn him over to you, and that's that."

He took a final pull on his coffee, set the cup down, and went back to his wanted posters, acting as though it were understood that I should leave now. Our discussion was over. Me, I sat there while he ignored me, finishing my own coffee as I tried to conjure up a way to beat him at his game, whatever it was.

"We got a wire saying there was a prisoner here to be picked up," I finally said. "You've got a telegraph office, don't you?"

"Sure we got a telegraph office," he admitted. "But I never sent for nobody from Twin Rifles. We take care of our own problems here, son. I don't need no outsider's help to run my town."

"Well, how about if you try that telegraph out and wire Twin Rifles on an official basis. You ask Marshal Carston if he doesn't want me to look into why his deputy is sitting in jail."

Forrest Haney scratched his head in thought before saying, "All right, son. I'll wire your town marshal and ask him just what you say. But unless he gets me official authorization to let that man go," he said, nodding toward Joshua, "he ain't moving a lick. Understand?"

"Sounds fair enough," I said, figuring I'd hear back from Pa inside of a day or so. "But I've got a notion you're gonna be real disappointed, marshal. Real disappointed."

"We'll see who's disappointed, son," he said as I left. "We'll see."

CHAPTER

★ 10 ★

Forrest Haney's coffee had stopped the growling in my stomach, but only on a temporary basis. I knew my next stop had best be the local eatery and a decent meal. I spotted a sign that boasted ANNIE'S PLACE on it and took a couple of steps toward it before stopping dead in my tracks. After the encounter I'd just had with Marshal Forrest Haney, I found myself holding the man in less than favorable favor, especially where letting Joshua go was concerned. There was something about the man that rubbed me raw, so I made one more detour before making my way to the eatery.

Annie's Place was slightly smaller than Big John Porter's cafe back in Twin Rifles. I couldn't remember ever counting the tables in the Porter Cafe but at first sight this place definitely looked smaller than the cafe Sarah Ann worked in. On the other hand, the smell coming from the kitchen suited the growl in my stomach just fine. Whatever it was, I hoped they served big helpings of it.

The cafe waitress smiled and showed me a table, leaving a menu and returning in a matter of moments with an empty cup and a pot of scalding hot coffee. From the way she looked over her shoulder when she first left, I got the idea she had already taken some kind of interest in me. But for the life of me I couldn't understand what it could be. Hell, I was unshaven and trail weary at best. How could that attract her attention? It wasn't but a minute or two after she'd poured my coffee and left that she was standing in front of my table, her head cocked to one side, apparently studying me in brief silence.

"Are you looking for something in particular?" I asked, looking up from the menu.

"Oh, pardon me," she said, coming out of her trance. Then, remembering who she was and her purpose, she added, "What would you like to eat?" Her pencil was quickly poised to take my order.

"I'll take whatever it is I smell in your kitchen," I said in my friendliest tone. "And coffee," I added, indicating the already half-empty cup in front of me.

"You must be hungry." Her smile reminded me a mite of Sarah Ann and I found my thoughts drifting to my wife.

"Ma'am, I've been hungry for the past fifty miles," I said in a serious tone. "Never got used to eating my own food."

She smiled at me as she once more cocked her head and took in my features, then wrote down my order.

She half turned to go, then stopped and faced me. "You know, mister, I like that smile of yours." She didn't wait for an answer, but headed back to the kitchen. It was a good thing she did too, for I suddenly felt my neck growing hot with what could only be blushing red.

Now, there goes a woman with a purpose, I thought to myself as I watched her walk away. Just what I needed, woman trouble.

It wasn't a minute later that she reappeared from the kitchen, carrying the coffeepot. As she poured more of the scalding liquid, she noticed I had pulled out the Colt Chance had given me. Actually, I was just studying the weapon to try and familiarize myself with it. I hadn't had that much time to do so on the trail up here. But then it crossed my mind that maybe this was a way to still this woman's sudden interest in me. What she saw was that I had opened the loading gate of my revolver and was slowly turning the cylinder, checking the rounds. "Now, what in the world is that for?" she asked in wonder. I didn't know whether she'd never seen one of these newfangled six-guns or if she flat out wasn't used to any of her customers fooling around with their guns while she waited on them.

"Well, ma'am, it was years ago that I visited one of those big-time eateries in Kansas City," I said with a straight face. "Ordered a piece of meat and specified it be well-done."

"Oh?" She said it with a tone of caution more than interest.

"Yes, ma'am. Found out the cook never heard of well-done meat. Why, they served me a piece of meat that was so red, it near bit me when I tried to cut it."

She smiled again. "You're joshing me, right?"

"No, ma'am," I said, finding it hard to keep on speaking with a straight face. "I had to shoot that piece of steer to make sure it was dead before they gave it back to the cook." Several of the customers who overheard this tale gave a chuckle. "That's why I always make sure I've got a sixth bean in the wheel before they bring out the meat in the cafe I'm eating in. Just taking precautions, ma'am, if you know what I mean."

She laughed, as did the customers who had been listening to the exchange. "You know, mister, I really do like that smile of yours. Why, I could take a liking to you real easy." Apparently, my story had backfired. Here I was wanting to get this woman to stand her distance from me and she'd just proven that she wasn't afraid of much after all. Least of all me.

A half hour later, I was still sitting there. The waitress had served a steaming plate of scrambled eggs, surrounding it with side dishes of baked ham, home fried potatoes, and a small, woven basket filled with biscuits and wrapped in a cloth to keep their freshness and heat. I had taken my time eating the meal, appreciatively thanking her each time she refilled my coffee cup. The truth of the matter was, I had hardly noticed her until an hour later, when she sat down across from me, placing a small plate of food before her as she took a seat.

The cafe was now empty except for the two of us. The fact that she had picked my table to sit at caught me off guard, for I wasn't prepared for it. Still, the young lady had a rather charming smile and was the first friendly face I'd seen in this town.

"Maria, let the man be." They were strong words

and had come from an equally strong-appearing man across the room. He stood a good six feet tall and, even with an apron draped from his neck, he looked as dangerous as Big John Porter. Or maybe it was the cleaver he held in his hand that added to the look about him. I found myself making an unconscious move to loosen the six-gun in my holster. Not once did my eyes leave the big man across the room.

"It's all right, Pa," Maria said, giving me a warm smile as she spoke. "I ain't bothering him." To me, she said, "Am I?"

"No," I said in a voice I'm sure she thought sounded a bit rattled. "I was just finishing my coffee. She's welcome if she likes." Maria heard her father return to the kitchen. She likely also saw the worry leave my face as the big man did.

"Forceful young lady, aren't you?" I said, taking a sip of the coffee.

Maria smiled. "Pa's always looking out for me."

"I got that impression."

Maria picked up her fork and knife and silently cut a piece of meat before she spoke again. "Well, you know my name. What's yours?"

"I didn't say."

"I know. That's why I'm asking." When I didn't answer her, she added, "I try to be friendly. In this business you have to. If you know what I mean." She gave me a half smile before taking a bite of her meal.

"Carston. Wash Carston," I said when she was half through her meal.

"Nice to meet you, Wash Carston," Maria said with a smile. I grunted and drank more coffee. This was just going to turn into more woman trouble. When I looked down at the cup, Maria made it a point to pick up the coffeepot sitting between us and refill my cup. Silently, I gave her a rather shy smile that conveyed my thanks.

Maria was almost finished with her meal when I pulled out a pocket watch and glanced at the time. A frown came to my face. I'd wasted precious time.

"Say, Miss Maria, you wouldn't know much concerning what goes on hereabouts, would you?" I said it in as casual a voice as I could, but it didn't surprise me at all when she stopped all movement and looked at me.

She slowly lowered her fork to her plate and said, "You're a lawman, ain't you?" She gave a quick glance at my chest, but didn't see a badge. Hell, it was still cold enough to keep my jacket on, so she couldn't have known anyway.

"Let's just say I work for the state." Sometimes people could shut their mouths right quick once they learned you were a lawman, so I wanted to get as many of my questions answered as possible before letting her know who I was.

"That takes in a lot of territory." Maria had suddenly lost all interest in her meal. When I looked into her eyes I knew. I had struck the same strange chord of terror in her as I had in Marshal Haney. But then they all seemed to have it in mind that Joshua was an outlaw and a killer, so it only seemed natural. What I didn't know was the relationship the woman before me might have with Haney or anyone else surrounding Joshua's case. I found myself hoping there wasn't one.

"I'm a deputy United States marshal," I said in a low voice. I leaned back and undid the buttons on my coat, letting it fall open so she could see the badge on my chest. "I'm looking for whatever information I can find on the fellow in jail now, name of Joshua Holly. Your Marshal Haney's telling me he's wanted for murder and I come to take him back."

Maria was suddenly filled with a combination of awe and fear. From the look of her she had never before seen an honest-to-God deputy U.S. marshal.

"Yes," she said when she'd finished staring at the badge I wore. "I know there's a man over there because I feed him his meals three times a day." She was quiet a moment before continuing. With a shrug of her shoulders, she said, "He seems nice enough for a man who's being charged with murder." She was looking down at her empty plate when she spoke, as though acting ashamed to be acquainted with Joshua.

When she looked up at me again, I was checking the rounds of my Colt again.

"You must be wanting that man awful bad," she said.

"It's my job, ma'am," I said, and if I sounded all business, it was likely because that's how I felt about getting Joshua out of the fix he was in.

"You on some sort of time schedule, are you? Train don't stop here, you know."

"No," I said with determination I hadn't caught in my voice before. "I just want to get it done and over with. That's what they pay me for." I found myself sounding a great deal like Pa, who had made the last twenty years of his life that of a lawman and took the job quite seriously.

I got up, sloshed on my hat, and loosened the Colt in my holster. It seemed to be a habit with me in situations like this. You never could tell who was going to show up and want to pick a fight with you. Not in a town like this, anyway.

"I didn't mean to make you mad, mister." The only thing that stopped me was the fact that Maria had taken hold of my hand and now held it firmly in her grasp. When I looked down at her, I thought I saw the pleading look of a woman who feared not for her life but for mine.

"Are you married?" I asked out of the blue.

The remark shocked her and she stood there wide-eyed. "Why, no. Why do you ask?"

"It sure seems to me you're looking for a man to push around," I said. "I swear, if I had my shirt tail hanging out, why, you'd be telling me to tuck it in." The words made her blush, but I didn't give her time to think or talk back. "Now if you don't mind, I've got some things to do."

I was at the door when I heard her say, "Wait."

I stopped, turned to face her.

"What is it?"

"I heard the other day that Randy Waite is involved in all of this," she said, a worried look about her. I didn't know whether it was worry she was feeling for herself or me. "The murder and all."

"What murder is that?" Suddenly, I found myself drawn to what she might have to say.

"Why, the man who was in jail before, the one they say was shot while trying to escape. They've got your man Joshua in jail for killing him."

"Is that right," I said, pushing my hat back and scratching my head, trying to figure out how confusing this was all going to get before it was over.

Then I was gone. Yes, sir. I had plenty of things to do this afternoon.

CHAPTER

★ 11 ★

My, what a surprise, Mr. Emmett," Sarah Ann said as the ex-cavalry sergeant entered the Porter Cafe. It was noon, a day after the Hadley Brothers had made fools out of themselves in the very same establishment. "I didn't expect to see you again so soon."

Emmett gave Sarah Ann a broad smile as his big hand swooped up and claimed the battered old cavalry hat on his head. The front brim of the hat was still folded back against the crown, pinned there with the miniature insignia of the crossed sabers of the cavalry. The man had gone through four years of war with that very same hat plunked on his head. Even after the war he continued to wear it, still proud of his onetime affiliation with the cavalry. "Why, shoot, missy, I've still got the quarter I was gonna spend on that steak yesterday." He shrugged, the smile growing wider. "But after your daddy told me the meal was on the house, why, I figured I ought to come back and spend it on a steak anyway. I'd feel plum guilty if I didn't, ma'am, I surely would."

What Sarah Ann liked about Emmett were the similar ingredients of her own husband's personality. Both men had manners and a sense of humor. She found her own smile growing as she led him to a table.

"What about your wife?"

"Oh, Greta's having tea with the Ferris women this afternoon," he said. "Gonna make a time of it, I reckon." He knew that most women, when they gathered on this frontier, would be hard put not to talk their fool heads off for the longest time. Of course, he also knew better than to admit to such knowledge to a member of the gentler persuasion.

It had been a while since Sarah Ann had made a social visit to Margaret and Rachel Ferris. She made a mental note to do so in the near future.

The noon crowd was beginning to occupy the cafe by the time Emmett took the first bite of his panfried steak. It was just as good as the one he'd had the day before.

"You managing, what with Wash gone and all?" he asked Sarah Ann around a mouthful of food, when she refilled his coffee cup halfway through the meal.

"As long as those Hadleys stay out of town I'll be all right, Mr. Emmett." There was a twinge of worry in her voice, but nothing so bad as she'd sounded like the day before, Emmett told himself.

"Not to worry, missy," Emmett said between bites. "I understand old Will give 'em a tongue lashing and swore to 'em he'd give up on words the next time they raised a ruckus like yesterday. I got a notion he means it too." Emmett gave Sarah Ann a confident smile and a wink before saying, "Don't you worry, Sarah Ann, they'll stay clear of you. Learned their lesson, that crew did."

Emmett enjoyed the rest of his meal and Sarah Ann seemed to perk up a mite after that. He was feeling so good then that he ordered a piece of Sarah Ann's deep-dish apple pie. It was when he was finishing the pie and polishing off another cup of coffee that Will Carston walked in and took a seat at his table.

"Have a seat, Will," he said after the lawman had already taken a position across from him.

"Just coffee, darlin'," Will said to Sarah Ann when she promptly appeared at the table. Both Sarah Ann and Emmett knew better than to ask Will if he wanted anything to eat. The man spent most of his mealtime eating at the Ferris House. And courting Margaret Ferris, some were saying. But Sarah Ann and Emmett knew better than to be the first ones to ask Will Carston his intentions toward Margaret Ferris. Courting was a man's private privilege and ought to be kept that way. It was town gossips who spoiled the suspense in a relationship like that. Sometimes even spoiled the relationship.

"Yes, Papa Will," Sarah Ann said with a hint of a blush and then was gone. She had always called her own father Papa and saw no reason to be different in her relationship with Will Carston, her father-in-law. The father of Wash Carston had taken to the name just fine, she noticed.

"Oughtta have some of this here pie, Will," Emmett

said, pointing a fork toward his now empty plate. "Some of the best I ever et." Then, lowering his voice and glancing around as though on the lookout for spies, he added, "Just don't tell Greta I ever said that. Woman'd kill me for sure."

Will smiled at Emmett, knowing well what the man meant.

Sarah Ann set down an empty cup and quickly filled it with coffee for Will. When she was gone, the marshal said, "Already had my fill for the day, Emmett." He took a good healthy sip of the steaming black liquid before adding, "Besides, I'm here more on business than pleasure today."

"Oh?" Emmett knew Will Carston to be one of the better storytellers he'd met along the way, and the two had shared more than their fill of lies and tall tales over the past year or two. But Emmett saw the man was in no storytelling mood at the moment, so his own disposition changed some too. "Something in the wind I should know about, is there?"

"That's a fact, Emmett. That's a fact." Will Carston was quiet for a moment, taking in more coffee as he seemed to mull over his next words.

Emmett grew impatient. "Well, spit it out, man! Just 'cause I got a farm instead of a ranch don't mean the work stops or slows down, you know," he said with a bit of temper showing.

"You recall that ride I sent Wash on?" Will said in a low tone of voice. This time it was he who looked around to see if Sarah Ann was anywhere in the vicinity. Emmett immediately found himself thinking that Wash was in some kind of trouble.

"Yeah."

"Well, I just got this over that newfangled telegraph we've got in town," Will said and pulled a folded piece of paper from his shirt pocket. Without opening it, he said, "It's from Wash. He found Joshua all right, but the local law has got the man in jail."

"Oh?" This single spoken word had a more than curious tone to it now. A worried frown also came to Emmett's forehead.

"For murder." Will said the words flat, leaving no doubt he was less than enthused over the idea.

"Jesus, Mary, and Joseph," Emmett said in a level as low as he could without letting out too much of the surprise he felt. No use in drawing Sarah Ann over to the table to get nosy about things. "What do you plan on doing, Will?" he asked in a concerned way. "Head out after 'em?"

Will pushed his hat back and scratched his head a mite before answering. "No. It's like I told Wash before I sent him. I've got these three yardbirds in my jail now and I'd just as soon not give 'em a chance to escape like they tried once before."

"Oh. Yeah." The three bank robbers had tried escaping once from Joshua's custody not long ago, but with little success. It was one of the reasons Will had chosen Joshua to pick up the additional prisoner when word had come he was ready to be picked up.

"What about Chance?"

Will shook his head. "He headed out toward that canyon him and Wash get their mustangs from. Left this morning. Said he'd be back in a day or two." Will cocked an eye at Emmett, adding a bit of a frown for effect. "And I can't wait two days."

Emmett felt something stir within him, something

he hadn't felt in quite some time. "You come asking for help, is that it, Will?" He couldn't recall the Carstons, any of the three of them, ever asking for help for anything, not since he'd been in Twin Rifles.

"Well, it's like this, Emmett. Other than my boys, I reckon the only ones I really trust with anything of this nature hereabouts would be you and Dallas Bodeen. Dallas, he's visiting some squaw he used to winter with back in the Shinin' Mountains, or I'd ask him, pure and simple." He paused again before saying, "I'd ask you, but you got that farm and all, and busy as you are, well, I reckon—"

"Oh, to hell with the farm, Will," Emmett said in his normal loud voice. "This is more important than that. Besides, most of the crops are already in. And Greta, why, she's got more preserving to do than she knows what to do with."

"I thought you were busy."

Again Emmett lowered his voice so what was said was strictly between the two men. "Truth of the matter is, Will, I've got more time on my hands than a gelded mustang. You got something you need done, you let me know and I'll do what I can." He added a wink and a nod to show his enthusiasm at helping a man who had been his friend since he'd arrived in Twin Rifles.

"I appreciate that, Emmett. I really do." A frown came over Will's face as he said, "But what about Greta? Do you think it's safe to leave her there all alone?"

Emmett gave off a belly laugh.

"Are you kidding me? Anyone tries to take over that spread, why, she'll likely scald 'em to death if she don't sic the kids on 'em. And they'll scalp the varmints, good as they're getting with a knife and a hatchet."

Before he could say anything else, Sarah Ann made a brief stop and refilled their coffee cups. The two were silent until she left.

"You're sure?" Will asked, a note of concern in his voice.

"I'm sure, Will," Emmett replied. Then, leaning across the table and lowering his voice, he asked. "Now, just what is it you've got on your mind?"

CHAPTER
★ 12 ★

Getting rid of that awful toothache was a real relief, I'll tell you. Of course, it had been replaced by a dull feeling in my left jaw that hurt a mite when I took to talking too much. I discovered that talking to the waitress Maria. But I reckon getting some decent food in my belly helped a lot too. And running into young Riley and Maria, well, they may have been the only two friends I had in this town. At least, they were the only two who had talked to me in a civil tone. Forrest Haney didn't seem too impressed with me; but then I wasn't too taken with him either, as tough as he talked. Still, I was finding things out and still had a lot to do before the day was over. Not the least of which was finding a place to lay my head tonight. Preferably a place with a fire nearby.

I pulled the collar of my coat up over my neck as I stood out in front of the cafe and glanced about, looking for a semblance of a hotel. So far I'd spotted a would-be church and been in the local law office, not to mention the saloon and cafe. I didn't recall seeing all that many individual houses in the area as I'd ridden into Sendero, so there had to be something resembling the Ferris House we had in Twin Rifles. Somehow, I couldn't picture everyone in this town spending their nights in the alleyways between the buildings. It just wasn't all that comfortable, especially in this weather.

About half a block down from Annie's Cafe was a sign reading MA STONER'S. As I approached the sign, I saw it was what I'd expected, what I was looking for. It was a good-size boarding house, boasting a VACANT sign in the window.

"Looks like you've got a customer," I said to the smallish woman behind the counter as I closed the door behind me. She could have been forty or fifty, I wasn't sure. In this land, it was hard telling a body's age. Mostly it depended on where you'd been in your lifetime and how hard you'd worked at being there. Her dirty blond hair was showing signs of gray in it, and her eyes were a soft, pale blue that looked like they'd seen a lot of people over the years. "I'd bet you're Ma Stoner too," I added, tossing my thumb over my shoulder at the sign outside.

"Well now, you can read and talk," she said with a hint of a worn smile. "Believe it or not, that's kind of rare in some of the men hereabouts."

I shrugged. "If you say so. I just want a room that's fairly warm at nights."

She spun her entry log around and pushed it toward me. "Too many lonely nights?" she said, the hint of a smile showing again.

I shook my head and returned her smile. "Too many cold nights."

"Rooms are four bits a night, payable in advance," she said in a businesslike tone. Before I could make any comment about the cost, she added, "That includes meals, of course."

She offered a pencil and I filled in my name, then turned the ledger back to her. She penciled in a number, turned, and grabbed a key off a board to her rear and handed it to me.

"You can have Number Two, just off the top of the stairs," she said as I took the key. "Don't have no potbellied stove in it, but it's right above the kitchen, so you'll be plenty warm most of the night, young man."

"Fine," I said, pocketing the key.

"Breakfast is served at six sharp; dinner at noon and the evening meal anytime between five and six at your convenience."

"That'll be fine, ma'am," I said and tipped my hat to her. I dug a silver dollar out of my pocket and tossed it to her. "In advance," I said, then headed back out on the street.

If you don't know who the town gossip is, just head for the saloon. I'd gauge that bartenders have heard more confessions than a priest, or run a close second. And the stories they hear are a lot longer than those a priest will come across. More time on their hands, I reckon. At any rate, I figured if anyone knew where I could find this Randall Waite that Maria had told me about, it would be the bartender.

As I crossed the street, I thought I saw young Maria, the waitress, making her way down the boardwalk from the cafe and ducking into the boardinghouse I'd just left. I could swear she was giving me some kind of secretive look as she did so too. I shook my head to myself and muttered "Women" under my breath. I've long had a notion that women will be the death of most men, and seeing this waitress sneaking into a boardinghouse on the sly only went to prove that line of thought.

Inside the Avalon, I didn't even have to ask the bartender for the whereabouts of Randall Waite. I took up the bar space near the batwing doors and began looking about as soon as I'd adjusted my eyes to the relatively dark interior of the bar. It doesn't seem to matter if it's a Mexican cantina or an American saloon, each and every one of them is as dark as a tomb inside. There must be something about drinking in the dark that enhances the taste of warm beer and poisonous-flavored whiskey for those who belly up to the bar. Maybe the men are all having a beer they secretively think their wives will never know about. I saw Randall Waite right off.

It wasn't the thick scar I noticed that ran across his jawline at an angle that led me to believe it was him. Nor was it the half-mean look he gave me when the bartender brought me a beer. Tall and lean, I'd seen his kind before. In a fair fight, Chance could have taken this man in no time, for my brother likely outweighed him by a good forty or fifty pounds. If this indeed was Randall Waite, he likely had a hideout gun or a knife stuck away somewhere on his body. His type always compensated for the odds against them.

It was his badge that gave him away.

Proud as a peacock he wore it, pinned to the left of the middle of his chest for everyone to see. It identified him as a deputy city marshal, and a one-horse town like this one couldn't have more than one deputy, two at the most. That's why I was sure this was Randall Waite.

He slapped the man next to him on the back and ordered up another whiskey for him.

"Why, thank you, my good man," the man said. He was in worse condition than I thought I'd seen the lad Riley a mite earlier. His hand was shaking some as he reached for the shot glass and downed it with little effort. "Now then, Randy," he said, addressing the deputy once he'd finished smacking his lips, "what is it you say is going to happen to our jailbird friend?"

My ears immediately perked up at the conversation they were having. There was only one man in the jail in this town and that was Joshua, and if it was he they were talking about, well, you can bet I was paying attention real quick.

Randall Waite motioned for the bartender with his hand, indicating another round of whiskey for the man beside him. "Don't you worry, Phil, I've got plans for the man. I've got plans that are gonna take care of him good."

"The s-s-sooner th' better, sir," Phil said, his speech a bit more slurred now. Apparently, I wasn't the only one who noticed it either.

"Don't you think that's enough, Mr. Turner?" the

bartender asked. His voice had a genuine note of concern for the man, who was obviously in no shape to do much but pass out any moment.

"Nonsense, Mr. Bartender, s-s-sir." The words were spoken with emphasis, but the slur was still evident in the man's drunkenness.

"Really, Mr. Turner, I think you need to call it a day," the bartender said, this time grabbing the bottle so it was out of Phil Turner's reach, as well as the deputy's. "You'd better head on home." To the deputy, he added, "Randy, why don't you give him a hand getting to his place?"

I could swear I saw a sly-looking grin cross the deputy's face as he passed glances between the bartender and Phil Turner. "No, I don't think so. I still want to hear what Phil has to say about our prisoner." It was evident the lawman had something other than the welfare of Phil Turner in mind. I was suddenly curious to see what it was, especially since it had to do with Joshua.

Abruptly, Phil Turner the drunk turned into Phil Turner the speechmaker. "I say we hang the sonofabitch!" he said in a loud, drunken voice as he turned to face the rest of the occupants of the saloon. He seemed to have everyone's attention too. "How many are with me?"

From the look of those in the crowd, I'd say that old Phil Turner had a pretty good chance of striking up the makings of a lynch mob, drunk or sober. My glance fell quickly back to the deputy as I wondered what he would do now. If the man did his job, he would be breaking up this lynch mob about now, making sure it never got formed in the first place. But he just stood there, leaning against the bar, looking in the mirror over the bar at the reflection of Phil Turner and the others in the saloon. The only determination I saw on his face was that of enjoying himself as he watched the whole scene develop.

He didn't plan on doing a damn thing!

"You'd better stop and think real hard, Mr. Turner," I said as I stepped away from the bar. Like I say, the insides of these places are dark and dank as can be, so being in a shadow of sorts was to my liking at the moment. After all, I didn't know how well he knew the others in the saloon. Maybe they'd follow him in a second, maybe they'd ignore him. I simply didn't know. Trouble was, I didn't want to find out the hard way either.

"And who might you be, young man?" Turner asked, his voice a bit more sober than a minute ago. Maybe sobering up was what he needed all along.

"A deputy marshal, just like your friend," I said in an even tone. "The difference is I know my law and he either doesn't know or doesn't care." I gave Randy Waite a hard glance and added, "Maybe both." His response was the same kind of threatening look back at me.

"And who are you to tell me what to do, stranger?" He seemed more alert now, as though ready for a fight.

I walked past the deputy and stood face-to-face with Phil Turner. If he wasn't drunk, he sure had the stink of a drunk about him.

"Believe me, mister, you'd do well to take my advice," I said with a frown and a growl, just to let him know I meant business. "You don't calm down and do it right quick, I'll escort you over to the jail. Awake or sleeping don't make no difference to me."

Either he was through talking or he couldn't think

of what else to say, for that was when he hit me across the face, knocking me back into the deputy. The blow only stunned me as I shook my head. That was the second time I'd gotten hit in this place today, and I don't mind telling you I wasn't any too keen about the idea. Fact of the matter was, it hurt like hell. Nor was I getting any assistance from Randy Waite, who did nothing more than push me back toward Phil Turner.

The only thing a drunk is ever good at is hitting a fellow from behind and hitting him with something big. Mostly, their own reflexes are so damned slow from absorbing all that Who-Hit-John that they don't have the force they might have were they sober. So when Turner swung at me again, I was quick enough to duck his blow and land a hard left in his side as I did. When he was gaining his balance and turning back to me, I smashed him square in the mouth and knocked him flat on his ass. He bounced on the floor, shaking his head to regain his senses.

"Mister, you're about to take a trip to the local jail for disturbing the peace," I said with a touch of meanness.

"Like hell," he muttered and, still lying there on the floor, went for his gun, which he wore in a cross draw on his left hip. I pulled my own six-gun—the first time I'd had occasion to use the Colt Conversion Chance had given me—and shot the pistol out of his hand. My Colt's aim was true, for I hit exactly what I was looking at. The bullet spanged off the metal of his own gun and the weapon went flying off to the side, Phil Turner grabbing his wrist in pain.

"You could have killed me!" he yelled. If he wasn't scared, he ought to have been. Hell, that Colt Conversion had let off one hellacious sound, which still left a ringing in my ears.

"Strange, I thought that was what you had in mind for me." I gave him a cocky smile, the kind I'd seen my brother flash on more than one occasion, and said, "All's fair in love and war, and believe me, friend, what you and I have is anything but love."

"But you could have killed me!" The scared was now turning to mad in the man.

"But I didn't. Now, get up and let's head for the jail."

He let go of his left hand and started to rise, stopping halfway to eye me. Then he got the widest damned grin on his face I do believe I've ever seen on a man. For the life of me, I couldn't figure out what he had in mind.

That was when someone dropped a rock that weighed a ton on my head and the whole world went black.

CHAPTER

★ 13 ★

It must have been past sundown when I came to in the jail cell next to Joshua. All I knew for sure was that my head hurt something fierce as I opened my eyes and looked about, seeing nothing but Joshua in the next cell.

"Take it easy, Wash," I heard Joshua say when I grumbled about the pain I was feeling.

"What I want to know is how I got in here," I said to anyone who would listen to me. No one said anything until I spotted Randall Waite, apparently standing guard over me as he took his seat at the marshal's desk.

"I reckon it's me who put you there, mister," he said, a leer on his face.

"Well, you can let me out now, deputy, for I said I was a deputy marshal too, and I meant it." I found myself getting good and impatient with the man. "Besides, you had no right to buffalo me like you did and jail me."

"Why, I sure did, friend," he said. "Here you come a-walking in and spouting off about being a deputy marshal, but not showing a thing in the way of identification. Just spouting off." He paused a moment before continuing. "Believe me, mister, I checked with Marshal Haney and he says you're lucky disturbing the peace is all you're being charged with now. So you just take it easy tonight and we'll turn you loose tomorrow morning, as long as you don't make a ruckus."

I was about to complain some more when I felt Joshua place a strong hand on my forearm and give me a cautious look. "Won't do you a danged bit of good, Wash, no good a-tall."

I sat back on my cot, once again shaking my head, hoping the ache would go away. "That being the case," I finally said, "why don't you tell me just how it is you come to be stuck in this place anyway, Joshua?"

"Well, like I said, Wash, it's a long story," he said.

I rubbed the back of my head and said in a soft tone, "I've got all night to listen to it, friend."

"It tends to get complicated after a mite, Wash, but I'll give her a go," Joshua said and proceeded to tell me what had taken place and why to his knowledge.

It turned out that Richards, the prisoner being held here that Pa had originally gotten the wire about, was in big trouble in Sendero. And it had been Maria, the waitress, and not the marshal who had sent the wire to Twin Rifles requesting that the prisoner be picked up.

87

"She brings the meals here three times a day and had caught on to this Richards being in need of help," Joshua said shortly. "With what I've been able to find out, Wash, Maria was figuring that this Richards character would have a better chance over to Twin Rifles, being jailed with his brothers and all, don't you know?" In an odd sort of way, I reckon it made sense.

The pain in my head was now more of a dull ache than the sharp suffering that had pierced my head when I'd first came to. The more Joshua spoke the more I was able to understand why he had wound up in jail here. Still, it didn't explain everything.

"But if you picked up the prisoner, how is it you wound up in jail?" I asked. On that matter, I was still confused.

"Actually, Wash, I didn't get a chance to pick up no prisoner," he said, continuing. "Why, they wasn't no prisoner to pick up. No, sir! Fact is, quicker'n a rattlesnake bite, they had me jailed up and charged with murdering the fella, can you believe it?"

"Murder?" If my tone sounded a good deal astonished, it was because that was how I felt. Hell, Joshua was no more a murderer than I was and both of us knew it.

"What they done, Wash, is railroad me the same as they have you," he said with a nod. "They just done it on a grander scale with me than you."

"Yeah, I see what you mean." Joshua was right too. I'd been slugged on the back of the head and jailed for supposedly disturbing the peace, while Pa's deputy had been jailed for nothing less than the murder of another prisoner.

"They're hiding something, bigger than God made green apples, you can bet on it," Joshua added, as though an afterthought.

"You won't get no argument from me on that," I said.

"The question is what?"

"Don't you worry, Joshua. As soon as I get out of here, I'm gonna make it my business to find out."

"Good for you, Wash," he said, his spirits obviously in better form. "Good for you."

My sleep that night was almost as fitful as it had been on the trail with that awful tooth. It seemed that the pain had simply been relocated to a different part of my body. I did my best to think of Sarah Ann, but all I could conjure up was trouble of one sort or another. If it wasn't Sarah Ann and her difficulty with the Hadley Brothers, it was Joshua being charged with a murder we both knew he didn't commit. I swear I couldn't find anything pleasant about the people in Sendero to think about, at least nothing that would put me to sleep or offer up pleasant dreams.

The dullness was still there the next morning when the sun rose and Marshal Haney arrived at his office a short time later. I found myself wanting a good cup of coffee and a decent meal in hopes that it would help satisfy my needs.

"Your deputy has got a jaded view of what the law is, marshal," I said when he picked up the keys to my cell and unlocked it, swinging the door wide open for me to leave.

"You want to watch talk like that, Carston," he replied in the same tough tone I'd heard the day before. "You're not out of my confines yet, you know."

"This may be your town, marshal, but I don't appreciate being treated the way I have been, not in any man's bailiwick," I said with a frown. My brother, Chance, is the one who is big on acting tough with those he confronts. Me, all I wanted this man to know was that I meant business. I just didn't tell him that my business in Sendero was far from over. "Hell, I was trying to stop the formation of a lynch mob, Haney. I wasn't anywhere close to disturbing the peace, as your deputy puts it."

Forrest Haney gave a noncommittal shrug. "If that's how you see it." He was quiet a minute as he gathered up his coffee cup and refilled it from the pot on the stove. "You know, Carston, you'd be a whole lot better off if you left town while you can," he said, a hard, even tone surrounding the words. I'd swear I saw what could only be an evil look in his eyes as he looked at me over a sip of his coffee. "Otherwise, you might not leave town."

There were no two ways about it. The man was threatening me, pure and simple. But I'd faced enough of those men to know that backing down from them isn't the way to deal with them.

"You tell your deputy if he tries to buffalo me again like he did last night, there will be hell to pay," I said as I picked up my Colt Conversion and checked the loads before holstering the revolver.

"I'm sure he'll be interested in hearing that, Carston," was his cold, calculated reply. No doubt about it, he was used to having his way. But then so was I to an extent.

I stopped at the entrance to his office, sloshing on my hat and putting on my coat.

"Come to think of it, Haney," I said through gritted teeth. "If you try pulling any trumped-up charges on me, I can guarantee you'll regret it the rest of your life. However long that may be."

Then I was gone.

CHAPTER

★ 14 ★

I made sure my first stop was Annie's Place. I wasn't sure that a hot meal ever cured a busted-up head but my stomach was telling me I might as well give it a try. Maria gave me another warm smile, silently showed me to a vacant table and handed me a menu. Enough of the tables were still filled with dirty dishes to indicate the breakfast crowd had come and gone.

"Where'd you disappear to last night?" she asked in a playful mood. "You missed a good supper meal."

"I imagine I'll hear the same from Ma Stoner," I said, doing my best to return her smile. "Stew, I think she said it was going to be."

"Probably. Most folks think she serves the best stew in town."

"I'm afraid I was a visitor of your local hoosegow." The smile grew harder to keep, especially when I remembered the fitful sleep and the manner in which I'd wound up in jail. "But as Pappy would put it, that's a whole 'nother canyon." It was the most tactful way I could think of to tell the young lady to mind her own business.

She did and took my order.

Young Riley entered the cafe and took a seat next to mine, giving me a silent nod and a hint of a smile as he doffed his hat and tossed it on the chair next to him.

"Rough night," was all he'd say, his words accompanied by a sheepish grin.

"Know what you mean," I replied.

After that, conversation sort of dried up and we each went about eating our morning meal. We were both sipping after-breakfast coffee when Maria approached my table. She seemed a bit shier than before, but for what reason I couldn't say. When she did nothing more than stand there like a bump on a log, I said, "Is there something I can do for you, ma'am?"

"Well . . . I was just wondering," she started to say, her words coming out in a halting manner.

"Yes?"

"Tomorrow's Thanksgiving, you know." She spit the words out, as though wanting to get rid of them in a hurry.

"Is that right?" The fact that Thanksgiving was coming up had crossed my mind only once, when I'd left Twin Rifles to come to Sendero. After that, things had happened too fast for me to have time to wonder about its existence.

She wrung her hands around the cloth usually stuck

in her apron before saying, "What are you doing tomorrow, Wash? I mean for dinner and all?"

I shrugged. "Couldn't rightly tell you, ma'am. Living life one day at a time is about as complicated as I get."

"Would you like to have dinner with us?" she said after a moment of worried hesitation.

"If he don't, I surely will, ma'am," I heard Riley say. Out of the corner of my eye I saw him giving her a fun-loving smile. How serious he was about it I didn't know. It struck my mind that his attitude seemed to have changed considerably since yesterday.

"That's real nice of you, ma'am," I said, feeling a mite awkward. After all, I was a married man. "Just who is *us*, if you don't mind my asking?"

"Oh." The word was accompanied by a hint of a blush. "It's the ladies in the church. The past few years we've been holding a big turkey dinner for those in town who care to come. Ever since they made it an official holiday, you know."

It was 1863 that Abe Lincoln and his crowd proclaimed the fourth Thursday of November the official celebration of Thanksgiving, a holiday of sorts. Before that it had been a day for feasting and prayers in remembrance of the Pilgrims and their early days at Plymouth Rock. Somewhere around 1621, I think Pa told us.

I gave her an embarrassed smile and said, "I reckon I can fit that into my schedule." What harm could having dinner with a bunch of Christian women from the local church be? If Chance were here I had no doubt he'd be the first to warn me that the only problem would be in explaining it to Sarah Ann. And he would likely be right. The woman loved me all right, but she could be downright jealous of my whereabouts and what I did at times. I knew she'd want a day-by-day description of what I did on this trip once I was back too. "Is there anything I should bring besides myself?"

"Well, we could always use another turkey," was her reply. Then she gave me that coy look a woman will conjure up when she's wanting something of a man. I'd be lying if I didn't admit to having seen it on Sarah Ann before. With a glance down at my Colt Conversion, she smiled and added, "I'm sure there aren't as many men around town who are as good at hunting as you are."

"I've got a rifle that shoots farther and truer," I said. "Who knows, maybe I can scare up some more game for your table this afternoon."

"Thanks, Wash, I really appreciate it," she said and leaned down and kissed me on the forehead. I think the kiss surprised her as much as it did me, for she quickly backed off as though she'd just touched her lips to fire.

Without a word she was gone.

I've got to admit, I was feeling some strange things then as I watched her move across the room to the kitchen. Some mighty strange things. Things you can bet I'd never tell Sarah Ann about, that was for sure.

"Nice-looking young lady, wouldn't you say?" Riley said and picked up his coffeepot along with his git-up end and planted both at my table.

"Yeah, I reckon you could say that." I finished off my coffee and pushed myself away from the table, leaving a coin in payment for Maria and for the invisible Annie, whoever she was. Then I planted my John B. on my head and left Annie's Place. No sooner was I out on the boardwalk than Riley was standing right next to me, trying to look as nonchalant as possible.

"Need a saddle pard? Or do you hunt alone?" he said when I gave him a sidelong glance. I figured I had a good decade on him when it came to age, so if I decided to, I figured I could treat him like some kind of pest. But I suddenly had the distinct feeling that he was wanting a friend in the worst way.

"I've hunted alone and in groups," I said as I headed for the livery. "I reckon one more in the party won't hurt." I only looked over my shoulder once on the way to the livery and sure enough he was there, right behind me. In a way, he reminded me of a brand-new puppy I'd had once way back when. Followed me around everywhere I went.

The old man wasn't anywhere in sight at the livery, so I saddled my own horse and Riley did the same with his. I remembered passing a creek outside of town, so we headed in that direction. Where there was water there was wildlife, and that was what we were after.

Approaching the area I had in mind, I reined in my horse and pulled out my Colt Revolving Rifle. A cap and ball rifle, I'd found it a good companion for me both during the war and after. I made sure all the caps were fresh and in place.

"Got a long gun, Riley?" I asked when my saddle pard did nothing more than check the charges of his six-gun, an 1861 Colt Navy Model, likely a .36 caliber. "Or do you plan on getting close enough to use your pistol?"

With no lack of confidence, Riley holstered his Colt

and said, "If it moves, I can likely hit it." He hadn't lost any of his cockiness, that was for sure.

All of a sudden he started coughing violently. I gave him a perturbed look and when he was through spitting out half of the contents of his lungs, he said, "Sorry. Hope I didn't scare off all the game."

"Ain't there no way you can stifle that coughing?" I asked with a frown. I was beginning to rue my decision to let him come along. Riley shrugged, shook his head, and spit some more in silence.

We rode without speaking for a while before coming on a clearing that looked as though it might house some turkeys. Dismounting, we made our way through some of the brush and stickers, trying to be as quiet as possible. I raised an eyebrow when I heard what I took to be a gobble coming from a turkey and froze dead in my tracks. I put a finger to my lips for quiet, and saw Riley take a deep breath, trying to hold his coughing back in the damnedest way. I gave him a hard frown, hoping he knew how important this was to me, getting these turkeys. But my luck wasn't to be and within seconds Riley was letting out a loud, boisterous cough that could have scared half the animals for a square mile around.

But turkey was all I was interested in at the moment, so even though I could hear deer and a couple other four-footed creatures making a hasty path in the opposite direction, it was the sound and movement of turkeys that held my attention. Two of them had been flushed, flapping their wings like mad and trying to put some space between them, us, and the sky above. I was hasty in my own movements and shot one of them through the neck with my first shot. I heard Riley's

Colt go off before I saw him move, and I saw the turkey fall to the ground, as dead as my own quarry.

"Lucky shot," I said as Riley coughed some more and spit out more phlegm.

He glanced at his pistol, holstered it, and said, "Luck ain't got a lick to do with it. Like I said, if it moves, I can hit it."

"Sure." I didn't press the argument about whether what he said was correct or not. It didn't seem right arguing with a man who was half sick all the time.

"Oughtta please those ladies at the church," Riley said and headed back to his horse.

We tied the turkeys to our saddles and took our time heading back to Sendero. Riley did more coughing then, followed by more spitting, in that order. Other than that, we were quiet most of the time.

"Your cough don't sound any better, Riley," I said after my saddle pard had gone through a particularly rough coughing spasm. "You sure you should have come out here and all? I mean, traipsing around like this? You sound like—"

"Yeah, I know," he interrupted, "I should be home in bed." The look on his face told me the man was in no mood to be coddled. "Well, for your information, Carston, I ain't got a home and I ain't got a bed. So mind your own damn business, will you?"

I shut up for a while as we rode on, but I still couldn't shake the idea that the man was in need of a friend. Maybe it was just what I'd seen in his eyes that one time. I was sure that he was putting up one hell of a front right now.

"My friends call me Wash," I said. When these words elicited no reaction, I added, "What do your friends call you?"

"Riley," he growled back at me, his mood not changed at all. "Not that it's any of your—"

The crack of a rifle shot sounded off to my right, but I didn't hear it until the bullet had gone whizzing close by my head. It must have looked awkward, but I dismounted as quick as possible, making sure my Colt Revolving Rifle was in my hand when my feet hit the ground. By then a second shot from a different gunman had taken Riley's hat off his head and he too was diving from his mount.

I wasn't about to waste ammunition, so when the horses wandered off, I tried to find the exact area the muzzle blasts had come from rather than shooting wildly at the bluff. But they stopped firing and were now mounting their horses and riding down the side of the bluff. I thought them lucky they didn't break one of the horses' legs, the way they were going. There looked to be three of them as they reached the flat land next to the bluff and tried to scurry away as fast as they could.

Riley had his pistol out, holding it with both hands as he took aim on them. I put a hand over his six-gun and shook my head. "They've got too much range for you."

Then, with my Colt rifle, I stood still and took aim on one of them and fired. They say Berdan's Sharpshooters used the Colt Revolving Rifle during the war. I didn't know how true that was, but I did know that I'd always choose this rifle over any other offered to me. The man threw his arms back, straightened in the saddle and slumped to the side, falling out of the saddle as his horse sped on.

"I hit what I aim at too, Riley," I said with a cocky smile of my own. "Damn near every time."

"That may be, hoss," he replied. Then, pointing to the man I'd downed, he said, "But that animal' tougher than you think he is." I followed his point of aim and saw what he was getting at. I wasn't sure where I'd struck the rider, but he was now getting to his feet as his compadres circled back and helped him up onto the back of one of their saddles. Then the three of them sped off on two horses.

"In that case, friend, you'd better mount up," said, taking good long strides toward my horse.

"Oh?"

"Yeah. Our hunting ain't done. Not by a long shot."

CHAPTER
★ 15 ★

By the time Riley and I had checked out the position my would-be assassins had fired from, they were nowhere to be found. Even from the height of the bluff, I couldn't see hide nor hair of them. But they did leave their calling card, if you want to call it that. And it was Riley who found it.

"Well now, looky here," he said as we looked the area over.

"Interesting," I said when he showed me the cartridge he'd snatched up from the ground.

"What do you figure, a .Forty-four-Forty? Likely from one of them newfangled Henry repeaters, I'd say," he commented.

"You'd be right then." The shell casing was indeed a

.44-40 that was most often used in the Henry Rifle. I had no doubt of this, for Pa had been carrying a Henry for some years now. "But there ain't much newfangled about 'em, I'm afraid. Henrys have been on the market for a good seven or eight years now. Seen a lot of 'em on both sides during the war."

"Figure it would be kind of hard to track this one down, do you?" he asked with a cocked eyebrow.

I nodded. "A lot easier than a Sharps, I'd say." Riley grunted something which I took to mean he knew what I was talking about.

"Oh, well," I said as we headed back to our mounts, "look on the bright side."

"Oh?"

"Yeah, we still got tomorrow's dinner meal"—I indicated the turkeys hanging from our saddles— "and we should be alive to enjoy 'em."

Riley began coughing again. When he was through spitting out his guts, he turned to me and frowned. "You mean *if* these other birds don't try potshotting you again before your turkey is taken off the spit."

"You're such a joy to be with, Riley," I said in my own growling tone. "I don't know why in hell I had you come along with me anyway."

He coughed and spit and grumbled some more, but kept it to himself for the most part. The rest of the ride back into Sendero was a peaceful one.

It was the middle of the afternoon by the time we pulled up to Annie's Place. Riley's cough had become about as quiet as the man himself; not that I missed it, you understand. I dismounted and handed my reins to Riley.

"If you want to take the horses down to the livery, I'll take these turkeys back to the kitchen," I said.

Riley mumbled to himself again, taking the reins grudgingly as he turned to the livery at the end of town. I made my way down the side alley and knocked on what I assumed was the side entrance to the cafe.

"Good," Maria's father said with a smile when he opened the door. "My daughter said you would be back with something for the dinner tomorrow."

"Happy to oblige," I said with a smile and handed him the birds. After a moment of silence, I added, "Riley and I missed the noon meal. I wonder if we could get a piece of pie and some coffee to tide us over until supper?"

"Sure. Just go around to the front and Maria will seat you."

"Thank you, sir." I tipped my hat and made my way back to the boardwalk and the entrance to the cafe. In the back of my mind I was wondering how good the pies were in this eatery compared to Big John Porter's cafe or the community table at the Ferris House, back in Twin Rifles. Shows you what a distraction will do to you.

I was about to open the door to the cafe when I heard dishes crashing inside. And before I knew it, the door was flying open in my face, knocking me back against the post holding up the roof over the boardwalk. It was the force of a big man that knocked the door open, and I saw him fall back past me as I got my senses back. I looked down at the sprawled body, then shook my head and squinted my eyes twice, not believing what I was seeing.

"Emmett?" Only one man I knew wore his John B. with the front brim pinned back by the insignia of the cavalry, and that was Emmett.

"Well, don't just stand there, boy," he muttered,

shaking his own head to clear the cobwebs, "give a man a hand." I reached down, grabbed him by the forearm, and yanked him up to his feet. Or maybe I should say I tried to yank him up to his feet. The next thing I knew, someone kicked me in the ass and sent me facedown on top of Emmett. We both grunted from the force of the blows to the other's body before I rolled off of him and onto my back. What I was looking up at was an awful mean, not to mention big, plug ugly.

"You do take 'em on big, don't you, Emmett?" I said, slowly getting to my feet. Like it or not, I had dealt myself a hand in this game, which was looking to be a crooked one if Emmett had tried to stop it.

Once I was on my feet, the man didn't look so big. Oh, he was an inch or two taller than me and outweighed me by maybe forty pounds, but then that pretty much fit the description of my brother too, and I could remember a time I'd beaten the hell out of him. So, this fellow, well, let's say he was going to be a chore at best.

I've gotten more bruises from Chance in the number of years we'd grown up together than anyone else I could recall. And if I learned one thing over those younger years, it was that you make do with what you have. In my case, I made up for lack of bulk with the speed I had. Just as Chance had big fists and a big frame, I found that I seemed to have natural speed in movement, which helped considerable when it came to taking on big pieces of rock like the fellow before me. I ducked when he threw a wide swooping roundhouse punch in my direction and missed me. When he got his momentum back, I hit him hard in the face a couple of times, but the blows didn't seem to phase him. All they did was jar him backward some. That was when I kicked him in his elsewheres. His face lost all expression and he sank to the ground, groaning as he held both hands over his crotch.

Emmett, on the other hand, took his fighting more seriously and was going at a second one with both fists flying. He had him up on the boardwalk, backing the man up against the front of Annie's Place as he landed one blow after another to the man's already bloodied face. The second fighter was sinking to the floor of the boardwalk when I saw a third, another big ugly one, come out of the cafe and look around, as though willing to take on whoever had dealt a hand in this brawl.

It was also then I saw Riley coming up the boardwalk from the livery, half running at a goodly pace. He stopped in front of the third man, gave the situation a quick survey, and swung two hard blows at the big feller standing before him. I'd bet a day's wages that the man outweighed Riley by a good seventy-five pounds! As for Riley's blows, they didn't seem to affect him at all. In fact, the look in his eyes said he was about to tear Riley in two within the next few seconds.

But if he was anything, Riley was quick on his feet. In that split second before the big man could move, Riley had his six-gun out and stuck right in the man's stomach. He slowly shook his head and said, "Don't even think about it, mister. It ain't worth it."

The words surprised Emmett as much as they did me, and he let go of the ruffian he'd been hitting, the man lifelessly slumping to the boardwalk. Then he tossed a glance at me, a frown on his face that said he'd sure like to know what was going on here.

"I'd listen to him, friend," I said to the big tough. "He tells me he don't miss much with that pistola of his. And truth to tell, I've seen buffalo that were thinner than you."

"All I've got to do is pull the trigger, mister, and you'll lie here dying and wondering all the while how could you be so damned stupid," Riley said. From the edge in his voice, I knew he was serious about gunning the man down.

"What the hell's going on here?" I knew it was Marshal Haney even before I saw him coming down the boardwalk. He too had a six-gun in hand, looking about as ready to use it as Riley. Before anyone could give an explanation, he shifted his point of aim to Riley and said, "Son, you put that gun away before I take it away and put you in jail for disturbing my peace."

Riley was dead set against the idea, maybe having the same opinion of Haney as I did and not wanting to let his guard down. In one quick movement, I reached over and relieved the ruffian of his six-gun before he knew it was missing. Then, silently, I nodded to Riley, hoping he'd take it as a sign he could holster his own six-gun without worrying about the local law jumping down his throat. He had a grudging look about him as his eyes darted between Haney and me, but Riley finally holstered his six-gun in as smooth a motion as it had come out in.

"I don't know who these three are," I said, handing the six-gun to the marshal, butt first, "but they seem hell-bent on trouble."

"That's a fact," Maria said, suddenly appearing in the doorway. "Marshal Haney, I don't want these men in this cafe until they can learn to behave proper."

"All right, Wade, let's you and your cousins amble on over to the jail," Haney said in a less than tolerant tone. "I've still got a cell that will fit all three of you." To me he said, "For your information, Carston, these are the Fraziers. Cousins, like I said."

"Kissing cousins, I'll bet," I heard Emmett say as he dusted off his weather-beaten cavalry hat.

One of the Fraziers made a move toward Emmett but before he could get far, Haney had an iron grip on the man and was leading him away toward the jail. Over his shoulder, he said, "I'll be back to get the particulars of just what started this, Miss Maria."

"Give these gentlemen some pie and coffee, Maria," her father said with a smile. In a lower voice, spoken just loud enough for each of us to hear, he added, "And don't let any of the three of them pay a dime."

"Yes, Papa," Maria said with a smile as the three of us followed her back into Annie's Place.

CHAPTER
★ 16 ★

And that's what happened, marshal. Honest." Maria reached over to the table next to ours and picked up her coffeepot and refilled our cups. Marshal Haney was true to his word and had returned to the cafe after locking up the Fraziers. He seemed to have a sense of just how important he was in this town too, for when he returned to the cafe he spotted us as soon as he entered and plunked himself down at the table Emmett and I were sharing. That was when Maria took a break and joined us, telling the lawman her version of what had happened in Annie's Place that afternoon.

"And you were doing nothing more than defending the young lady's honor, is that right?" he said to

Emmett, casting a suspicious eye on the stranger as he spoke.

Emmett held up his right hand, as though preparing to take the oath in a court of law. "I'll swear to it on anything you call a bible, marshal. The Good Book, a case of whiskey, your mama's grave, you name it," Emmett said sincerely. "But that's exactly what I was doing. Yes, sir." He pressed his fork down on his near empty plate, picking up the remaining few crumbs of the piecrust he could spot and savoring the last of his pie. He'd done the same with the first piece of apple pie Maria had served, and it had apparently impressed her—or flattered her—enough so she'd brought out a second piece for the man.

Between Maria and Emmett, I got the notion that the Fraziers were Sendero's variation of Twin Rifle's Hadley Brothers. It was just that in this town trouble ran to cousins and not brothers.

Apparently, the Frazier Cousins—Jethro, Hanson, and Wade by name—had swaggered into Annie's Place bold as you please and decided to all but take it over. Like I said, they were big ones, nearly as big as John Porter I'd gauge. But the sameness ended there for where John Porter was an intelligent and generally peaceable man, these three were belligerent as hell. They'd started bragging and boasting, raising hell in general, to hear Maria tell it, grabbing at the waitress once or twice. But Maria wasn't having any of it that day and threatened to pour a goodly amount of steaming hot coffee over Jethro's wrist if he didn't let go. When she began to make a move to follow through on what she'd said, he'd let go of her like she was some hot potato.

"It wasn't a minute later that Maria was carrying

out another pot of coffee and that damned jackass made another grab for her," Emmett said, a frustrated look about him. "Well, let me tell you, son, I'd gone through that routine once before back in Twin Rifles and it ruined my meal. Surely did."

"What did you do?" I asked.

"Why, I yelled out 'Boots and saddles!' and charged the stupid bastard," he said, ramming a fist into the palm of his other hand for effect. "Grabbed that first one, Jethro I reckon it was, by the stack and swivel and proceeded to toss him out of the establishment."

"You say you proceeded to throw him out?" I frowned. "As I recall, it was you who came flying out in my face, wasn't it?"

Emmett suddenly had a sheepish look on his face. "Well, I didn't quite proceed with what I intended to do. Let's put it that way." It turned out that Hanson Frazier had shaken Emmett loose from his grip on his cousin Jethro, and turned the tables on him, tossing Emmett out of the cafe instead. From there on I had a pretty good idea of what happened, for I was a part of it then myself.

"That sounds like their style," Haney said with a nod, apparently satisfied that Maria and Emmett were telling the truth. "I'll keep 'em in the hoosegow overnight and warn 'em not to come around Annie's and to behave themselves in town."

"You sure you can't keep them fools locked up a might longer, marshal?" Riley asked, a look of concern crossing his face. It was the first time he'd spoken up since the lawman had planted himself at our table. Not that I could blame the man, for the Fraziers had been anything but easy to take care of, and doing one in with a six-gun might have ended all of his problems but it would have been the start of a whole passel of trouble for Riley. I reckon he knew as well as I did that this lawman was big on locking up murderers.

Forrest Haney smiled for the first time I could remember since meeting him. But then he was looking at Maria when he smiled so that explained that. And Maria was anything but ugly. "I would if I could get away with it, but I've got a notion Ma Stoner will be paying me a visit to make sure I let all of the overnight drunks out of jail for her doings down by the church."

"Oh, that's right," Emmett said, snapping his fingers as though remembering something important, "it's Thanksgiving Day, ain't it?" To me, he added, "I hope you appreciate what I'm doing for you, Wash."

Without another word, Forrest Haney tipped his hat to Maria, bid us good day and was gone.

"You say you had some trouble back in Twin Rifles over a meal, Emmett?" I asked when the local law was no longer in sight. As soon as he'd made that comment, I began wondering how Sarah Ann was doing and whether it was any better than Maria had been faring with her customers.

"Fact of the matter is, Wash, I did," he said and set about telling me about his run-in with the Hadleys and how they had tried to do damn near the same thing with my wife as the Fraziers had with Maria. Their intentions, though, were much worse, to hear Emmett tell it. Then, all of a sudden, the ex-cavalry sergeant broke out in laughter. Pure, gut-busting laughter. Me, I wasn't sure what it was that brought on the fit of hilarity. But his laugh had managed to attract Maria toward our table again.

"What's so funny?" she asked, warming up our coffee. I think she was as confused as I was.

111

Emmett almost had tears coming down his cheeks before he could stop laughing.

"You know, Miss Maria, what you did to those Fraziers, warning 'em and all, that was fine," he said, now grinning from ear to ear. "But I've got one other trick you can add to your repertoire."

"Oh?"

"Yeah. You see, Wash has a wife back in Twin Rifles and she's a waitress just like you," Emmett said. He then proceeded to tell of how Sarah Ann had handled the Hadleys by tossing a pot full of steaming hot coffee into the lap of one of them. "I swear old Carny Hadley is gonna be walking real gentle the next few days," he added with a chuckle. "Tamed that boy real good, she did."

I felt myself let out a sigh of relief now, knowing that Sarah Ann had done quite well in standing up for herself against the Hadleys. Of course, I was just as thankful that Emmett was there to stop the Hadleys when he did and mentioned it to him.

"That's all right, Wash," he replied, giving me a slap on the back and a welcome smile, "that's what neighbors are for, ain't it? Besides, I know that you'd have done the same for Greta if she was between a rock and a hard place."

I didn't have to think twice to know that what he said was true. You didn't get far in this land without helping out your neighbor and putting the same kind of faith in him that he put in you. I reckon it was just an unwritten rule of the land, something that was inborn in you as you grew up with the land and the country.

Riley, who I'd almost forgotten about, coughed

some and spit to the side. "Looks like you got some real stand-up friends, Wash," he said in a soft voice.

I looked at Emmett and gave him a friendly smile. "Yeah, Riley, I reckon I do."

"I'd have killed the sonofabitch," Riley said matter-of-factly. "I'd have killed all three of 'em. Just like I almost killed the one today." I could only guess that he was talking about the Hadley Brothers.

Emmett shook his head in disbelief, not quite sure what to make of this young lad. Me, I'd known him all of a day and a half so far, so maybe I had more insight into him than Emmett did.

"Yeah, Riley, I'll just bet you would have too," I said.

CHAPTER

★ 17 ★

If the weather had been warmer, I'd have propped myself up in a chair on the boardwalk and taken in the town of Sendero the rest of the afternoon. With all that pie and coffee Maria had served up, I could easily have fallen asleep for an hour or two until suppertime. But it was easy to see that fall was quickly dying away, replaced by an early winter season and some mighty cold winds blowing into the area. I wondered if they were feeling this kind of cold yet back in Twin Rifles.

"Where can a man find a place to lay his weary head at night?" Emmett asked, pushing himself back from the table and patting his belly, now full of more pie than either Riley or I had eaten at this sitting.

"Ma Stoner runs the boardinghouse in town," Riley volunteered before I could get a word out. "Pretty nice place if I do say so." In a way it surprised me, Riley being this open with anyone since finding out he had consumption. But when he went into a coughing spasm and spit into the far corner, I was brought back to the reality of what the man was really like.

"You got a room at Stoner's?" I asked in a slight tone of awe.

"Sure do." With a playful wink, Riley added, "If you spent a night there once in a while you'd find out."

Emmett looked at me in mock surprise. "Good Lord, boy, just what is it you've been doing with your nights in this town?" he said as we left the cafe. "Come on, Wash, tell me all about it. I've got to have something to tell Greta so she can tell Sarah Ann."

"You think I want to die young, do you?" I said on the boardwalk. It was only a short walk to Ma Stoner's place, but I buttoned up my jacket anyway. As the day progressed I noticed that the wind had gotten colder and stronger as it blew through Sendero. "Let's get you a room at Stoner's and I'll explain the situation to you."

Young Riley tagged along. I still had a notion the lad was looking for a friend awful bad. Or maybe it was the pie that eased his line of thought. Food has been known to do worse to a man.

"I'm gonna take a nap," Riley said when we were inside the Stoner boardinghouse. "Wake me when supper is served." He didn't wait for an answer, simply made his way up the stairs and opened the door to the room right at the top. That put him right next to me. I reckon he had some warm nights too.

"Strange young man, wouldn't you say?" Emmett said, also watching Riley disappear into his room.

"Now don't you go judging him too harshly, boys," Ma Stoner said from behind the counter. "He has his moments, just like all of us."

"If you say so." I wasn't about to argue with the owner of this establishment, what with the wind being what it was outside, even if she was a woman.

Emmett got signed into a room about two doors down from me, then went to get his gear off his horse, which he'd left down at the livery stable. With a promise to be right back, I stood there leaning against the counter, just me and Ma Stoner. But if it was quiet I was expecting, I was sadly mistaken.

"And where were you last night, young man?" she asked in a brisk tone as soon as Emmett had closed the front door.

"Is that why they call you Ma?" I asked in as civil a manner as I could muster. The tone of her voice and the stern look on her face reminded me an awful lot of my own mother and the way she'd taken after me when I was a youth.

"Why, of course," she replied with what I took to now be a pleasant smile, seemingly not embarrassed at all. "Now, where did you say you were?"

I explained to her the episode of what took place in the Avalon Saloon, my run-in with Randall Waite, and how I wound up in jail for the night. I also tried to keep from blushing my own self when I told it. No man likes to look the fool if he can help it.

"You want to watch yourself around Randall Waite," she said when I'd spoken my piece. "He's a dangerous and bad man from what I hear. Mark my words." A harsh shake of the finger went along with her testimony.

I was about to ignore her when her last words caught my attention. That was when it hit me. This woman may be as close to a town gossip as I'd ever find. And what better place to gather information, even if only in the form of a rumor, than from a town gossip. Odds were you wouldn't find anyone else qualified to know so much about the town's comings and goings.

"Tell me, ma'am, what do you know about the man the marshal has got in jail now?" I asked. "The one they're holding for murder."

She picked out a spot on the other side of the room, staring at it momentarily, as though it would conjure up the words she was needing. "I don't know, really. But I'll tell you this much, there's something awfully fishy about that whole situation with Marshal Haney and that upstart Randall Waite."

"Oh?" Suddenly, I couldn't have cared less if she was the town gossip or not. She had what sounded like some information I could use to get Joshua out of jail, and the truth of it was I could use all the help I could get.

"The whole thing is a mess, if you ask me. I mean, the marshal comes on this man who is known to be wanted somewhere else for a bank robbery. They jail him and he's only there for a week before he's dead. Just like that," she said with a snap of her fingers.

"No explanation at all?" The more I found out about this difficulty, the less I seemed to know about it.

Ma Stoner shook her head. "None whatsoever."

"That is strange."

"Until that young man now sitting in the cell arrives in town. Then this other man suddenly disappears, buried in boot hill on the outskirts of town, they say. Shot by the young man over there in jail." A frustrated look came over her now as she tried her hardest to remember something. "Oh, phooey! There's something that stuck in my mind about that situation that I can't remember." A disappointed grunt only emphasized the tension she must be feeling. "Don't worry, lad, it'll come to me. And when it does I'll tell you."

When Emmett returned we gathered up a couple of chairs and sat around the potbellied stove, filling each other in as we waited for supper to come around. I told Emmett the story of my stay overnight in the hoosegow, a story I was getting tired of retelling already. And Emmett told me about Pa and his worry over what might have happened to me, not to mention Joshua, and why he'd sent Emmett to check on both of us.

"Just what the hell is going on around here, anyway, Wash?" he asked. "It isn't too often I ride into a town and run into a fight first off. Why, the last time something like that happened was when I first rode into Twin Rifles a couple of years back."

I tried to explain to him as best I could what I'd found out and what I thought had happened. Not being able to talk to Joshua didn't help much. And what I'd found out on my own didn't add much to the story either. For one brief moment I thought about relating what I'd just found out from Ma Stoner, but passed it over as a bad idea, confusing at best. Besides, clear heads were what was needed now.

It was a little after dusk when we decided to call it a

day. I was in my room, unstrapping my gun belt when I heard a light knock on the door. I must have had a surprised look on my face when Maria saw me for that was exactly how I felt at the sight of her.

"What are you doing here?" I asked with just as much surprise.

"Oh, I just brought those turkeys you and Mr. Riley shot over to Martha for tomorrow's meal," she said with a warm smile. In fact, I'd have to say it was a whole lot more than friendly. I had a surprising uneasiness in the pit of my stomach when she said those words. Somehow, they didn't ring true.

"That gave you a reason to stop by and see me, did it?" Keeping my composure didn't seem to be the easiest thing to do at the moment, and I was damned if I knew why.

She shrugged, then put an arm out and leaned against the door in what I reckon was supposed to be a sultry type of pose. The smile was still there when she said, "I was talking to Martha and she mentioned that prisoner they got over to the jail." Martha, apparently, was Ma Stoner's first name. "Said you were as curious about him as she is."

When she fell silent, I said, "And?" with a bit of impatience.

She leaned forward and, without any warning—which was how it was supposed to be, I reckon—kissed me on the lips. Hard, and with what I took to be a good deal of passion. I couldn't tell you why I didn't back away sooner than I did. All I knew was that Sarah Ann would shoot me if she ever found out about what was taking place now.

"No, ma'am," I said as I pushed Maria away at arm's length. "Maybe I ain't wearing a ring and all, but you can take my word that I'm a married man. That's a fact, ma'am."

Maria's smile turned suddenly devious. "But you liked it, didn't you? I could tell."

"Listen, Maria, you can't just go around kissing any man you like," I stammered. "Why, it ain't done. Not if you want to live to a ripe old age. Especially if my wife finds out."

"But you liked it, didn't you?"

"You just git, ma'am, before I help you down the stairs with the toe of my boot!" I didn't figure I could get much more emphatic than that.

She turned to go and as I looked over her shoulder I almost had apoplexy. There, at her counter and in full view, was Ma Stoner taking in both of us as we acted like fools!

"By the way," Maria said as she stopped at the head of the stairs. "Martha said she remembered what it was she forgot."

"Do tell," I said, suddenly forgetting our earlier confrontation not a minute ago.

"That prisoner that got killed and disappeared all of a sudden?"

"Yeah."

"If he got shot while trying to escape, he never got any farther than his jail cell door. His leg was broken in two places, and I ain't seen a body yet that could get far with that much of a busted-up limb."

"Are you sure?" I said in pure amazement.

"I ought to be," was her reply. "I fed him three meals a day while he was alive. And that busted-up leg was hard to miss."

CHAPTER
★ 18 ★

Damn it, Carny, I'm tired of being run out of town."
Ike Hadley was the youngest of the Hadley Brothers
and eagerly wanted to follow in his bigger brother's
footsteps, which likely brought on his outburst.

"Calm down, Ike," Wilson Hadley said. "Ain't
Carny or me likes it any more than you do."

"Then let's go back into Twin Rifles and take old
man Carston apart," Ike growled, pulling his six-gun
out and checking his loads. "I say let's teach him a
lesson."

"Now, Ike, you listen to me," Carny said in a stern
voice to his younger brother. "First thing you do is put
that pistol of yours back before you go shooting

yourself. Then you do like your brother says and calm down some."

It had been at least two days since the Hadleys had their run-in with Sarah Ann and Emmett at the Porter Cafe, maybe more, Carny wasn't sure. All he could remember was that feisty little waitress pouring most of a pot of hot coffee into his lap. In fact, the only other thing he remembered was Will Carston running the three of them out of town once the fighting was all over. And that ex-cavalryman Emmett, why, he sure was glad he wasn't in his unit during the war. The man had a mean streak that came out in him when he took to fighting. Of course, those ham-size fists didn't help either. Lordy, could he hit a wallop.

Ike Hadley grudgingly took a seat at the table in one of the hard wooden chairs located about the cabin they lived in. The cabin served as their living quarters but was nothing like the ranch house Wash and Chance Carston now had. This cabin had been a long time since last experiencing a woman's touch.

"Well, what are we gonna do then? We've got to do something, don't we?" Ike said, still frowning. He had a pretty good idea that Carny wasn't going to do much of anything until he felt he could get around again. But what about him and Wilson? Couldn't the two of them go back into town and give hell to the marshal? It sounded like a pretty damn good idea and he said as much to his brothers.

Carny's head shot back in surprise and this time it was the older brother who took on a frown. "I was you, I'd watch myself, Wilson," he said. "Sounds to me like your younger brother's brains just dribbled out his ears."

Wilson nodded agreement. "Either that or he's taken a stupid pill."

"A stupid pill?" Ike wasn't sure what Wilson was talking about. The confused look on his face said so.

"You just get that idea out of your head, little brother," Carny said with a note of finality.

"But damn it, Carny, I'm telling you we got to do something," Ike started to reply. He never got any further for it was then that his older brother reached across the table and slapped him hard across the mouth.

"Let's git something straight here and now, Ike," Carny growled in a nasty tone, nastier than Ike had heard him speak in a long time. "It'll be a cold day in Hades before you start telling me to do anything, understand?"

Slightly younger than Wash Carston, Ike Hadley had never felt the individual confidence that the younger Carston had shown since coming back from the war. He'd been fine while Carny and Wilson had been away, fighting for the Confederacy, for there had been only himself and his mother to take care of. And Mama had appreciated every little thing Ike had done for her. But then she'd died a year before the end of the war and Ike had felt so alone in the world it was pitiful. It was when Carny and Wilson showed up after the war that they took to bullying him, just like they had before. Any confidence Ike might have had was suddenly gone for his brothers had once again taken over. Finally, he had decided to be like them and used the anger building up in himself to fuel what he felt. He felt he could fight at the drop of a hat, but not his brothers. He simply couldn't build up the courage to face them.

"I understand," Ike said in a much softer voice, wiping a trickle of blood from his lip.

"Just what do you have in mind, Carny?" Wilson asked when silence fell over the three of them.

Carny tenderly scratched the inside of his thighs, knowing neither one of his brothers would make any comment on his misfortune for he was bigger than either of them. When it became clear that his mind was in some kind of deep thought, both of his brothers did little more than look at one another and shrug, waiting for their brother's words of wisdom.

"I ain't for sure how I'm gonna do it, but you're right, Ike, I'm about as tired of being run out of Twin Rifles as you and Wilson are," Carny finally said. What had happened the other day in the Porter Cafe wasn't the first time the brothers had been run out of town. In fact, it seemed as though every month or two the lot of them were involved in some kind of mischief that eventually got the attention of Marshal Will Carston, who would warn the Hadleys to stay out of town until they could behave themselves. Then, in another month or two, the cycle seemed to start all over again. And all because the three of them liked a little fun once in a while.

"Good," Ike said, eagerly rubbing his hands together, a willing smile on his face. "We're finally gonna get back at those Carstons."

"Now, you just hold on, Ike," Carny said, once again taking on that stern tone in his voice. "What we do we're gonna do my way, understand?"

"Sure, Carny, I understand."

Carny squinted up his eyes as though still in thought before saying, "What I got in mind you may find a mite strange."

Wilson shrugged. "Hell, I'll try anything, you know that. Long as we can keep that marshal off our backs."

"That being the case, I figure they's only one man can help us," Carny said.

"Who's that?" Ike asked, once again brandishing an eagerness about his brother's words.

"Pardee Taylor."

Ike's smile was a gratifying one, for although he hadn't seen Pardee Taylor in some time now, he remembered him as the town bully and practicing town drunk.

Wilson Hadley slowly shook his head, not sure what to make of his brother's words, nor the idea behind them.

CHAPTER
★ 19 ★

In a way it seemed odd, but my sleep that night was about as discomforting as the night I'd spent on the trail with that bad tooth. Oh, I fell off to sleep quick enough. It just seemed that I couldn't stay in one spot in that bed. I tossed and turned, wondering at first if what Maria had said about that prisoner having a leg broke in a couple of places was the truth or some tall story she'd invented after giving me the business in the doorway. Finally, I put it out of my mind, knowing that I had all day tomorrow to think on it. Besides, I had an actual bed to sleep in for a change, not the hard ground or that lumpy cot in the lawman's jail cell. And Martha, if that indeed was Ma Stoner's real name, had been right about the room; being located over the kitchen like it was, it provided a fairly warm feeling for what might otherwise have been a cold room.

When I finally did sleep I had some strange thoughts running through my mind. I couldn't help but think of Sarah Ann and how I missed her, so you'd think I'd dream about the woman. But no sooner did Sarah Ann enter my dream than she—or at least her face—was replaced by Maria, the waitress at Annie's Place. And all she had on her face was that coy smile I'd seen on her in the hallway as she leaned against the door to my room. Then she started walking toward me, still smiling that smile. Me, I kept on backing away from her, knowing how proud Sarah Ann would be of me when I told her how I'd fended this creature off. But I wasn't to succeed at it, and soon Maria was right before me, holding her arms out to me until she had them around me. And once that happened she leaned forward to kiss me and . . .

I woke up in a cold sweat. Sat straight bolt upright in my bed, I did. The room was suddenly cold, any semblance of warmth now gone. It was pitch-dark outside when I glanced at the lone window in my room. I laid back down and closed my eyes, but sleep was gone for the night and all I could do was lie there and wonder at the dream—or was it a nightmare?— I'd just had. I lay like that for nearly a half hour before taking another glance at the window. This time I saw that gentle haze of light that appears out of nowhere when the sun is about to make its debut for the day.

I pulled on my pants, boots, and hat and was strapping on my gun belt as I closed the door behind me and made my way down to the first floor. The only light available came from the kitchen area, so I wandered back there. The closer I got the stronger the smell of brewing coffee became. As I slowly pushed open the door, I saw Ma Stoner busying herself over a stove with whatever combination was being put together for the day's morning meal.

"Coffee smells good, Miss Martha," I said in a soft voice.

Still, she jumped at my words. "Oh! You scared me, son."

"Thought I made enough racket coming down the stairs." I smiled to let her know I was harmless this early in the morning, even without my coffee.

"By the time you pull a cup out of that cupboard over there, the coffee will be ready, Mr. Carston," she said, regaining her composure and going back to her work.

"You can call me Wash, ma'am. Most of my friends do." With cup in hand, I grabbed a spare pot holder and poured myself a cup of the hot black stuff. And Lordy was it good! But then the first cup usually is.

"I'll bet you know the name of that young waitress over to Annie's too," she said, making no bones about what looked all too much to be her matchmaking skills.

"Sure. Maria."

"She's taken a liking to you, you know."

"I got that impression last night." I almost choked on the next swallow of coffee as the red crept up my neck. I reckon it was the all-too-vivid memory of Maria and last night that caused it. I think. "But I'm married, Miss Martha. You know that, don't you?"

"Oh?" She turned away from her chores for a moment to take in my hands, my left hand in particular. "Hmm. I didn't think I saw a wedding band on you. Claiming they're married can get real convenient for some men who don't want to be bothered."

"Not me, ma'am," I said with a firm shake of the head. "It's been a year and a half now I've been married to Sarah Ann." Martha's face still held a doubting frown as she glanced again at my ringless finger. "I reckon breaking horses ain't the most profitable way to make a living in this world," I added with a sheepish grin. We never did have enough money scraped together to buy the proper rings; Sarah Ann knew that would come later, when I had enough money to be able to afford it.

Martha took in the features of my face, then grabbed my left hand and opened it, feeling over the callouses that Sarah Ann complained about sometimes.

"I guess you are telling the truth, son," she finally said.

"He wouldn't have it any other way, ma'am," I heard Emmett say from the entrance to the kitchen. His hat had been planted on his head at a cockeyed angle and he was just pulling his suspenders up and over his shoulders. "You don't mind if I, uh . . ." He nodded his head toward the coffeepot. For as blustery as he could get, he could be downright humble at times, a fact which could sometimes be confusing.

"Go ahead, go ahead," she said in a perturbed manner, waving a hand about. "I've got work to do here and it's gonna have to get done right quick if I'm to feed my customers."

"Well, ma'am, you let old Emmett and Wash know what we can do for you, and by Harry we'll do it,"

Emmett said emphatically. If he hadn't had a hot cup of coffee in his hand, I reckon he would have been even more ambitious in his voicing.

"Well, I can always use more wood. There's some out back in the hamper, if you'd care to bring a load or two in."

"That'll be just fine, ma'am," Emmett said. He turned toward the door, then stopped and turned back toward Martha. "By the way, ma'am, just out of curiosity, what is it you're serving for breakfast this fine morning?"

"Flannel cakes, ham, and fried potatoes. Biscuits and honey on the side," she said and went back to her work.

Emmett's eyes lit up and he gave off a broad smile. This woman had found the way to his better side. "Wood. Lots of wood. Coming right up, ma'am. Yes, ma'am," the big ex-cavalryman said and rushed out into the cold of early morning, coffee cup still in hand. I had a notion he'd be balancing the cup on the deadwood when he returned.

"Anything I can help with?" I asked, although I couldn't for the life of me see anything that needed doing. This woman seemed to have a handle on it all.

"Grab up some of those potatoes and wash 'em off for me," she ordered. "I'll be frying 'em up soon."

I did what she requested and was silent for a few minutes as Emmett made a trip in, arms full of firewood. Actually, I had no qualms about helping Martha out at all, for it was me who had done most of the cooking when Chance and I were on the trail together, or even in our bachelor days after the war, when we'd lived at Pa's old ranch house. My brother knew weapons and ammunition all right, but he couldn't make a meal to save his life. Couldn't find a pan to boil water in if he had to.

"Maria was telling me last night about that prisoner having a busted leg and all," I said when the potatoes had been scrubbed clean.

"That's right," she said, turning away from her work. "That was what I couldn't remember yesterday." With raised eyebrow, she added, "Ain't seen a man yet who moved too well with a twicet broke leg."

I nodded in agreement. It was something to think on and you could bet I'd do my share of it. Maybe even ask a few questions about it.

Back at cooking, Martha looked over her shoulder and said, "You know, Wash, Maria is gonna need an escort to the church service this morning. The circuit rider promised he'd be here for the holiday, and sure enough he showed up yesterday afternoon." Which shows you how distracted a body can get when he has things on his mind, I reckon. I couldn't recall seeing him ride into town at all.

"Can't her father take her?"

"Oh, heavens no! Between Harry and me, we'll both be cooking up I don't know how many turkeys and such," she said with a chuckle. "Besides, Harry will tell you we're both too old for religion. Religion is for learning while you're young enough to grasp it. Get old enough, like me and Harry, why, you're lucky to remember it, much less practice it."

"And you want me to take her?"

"If he don't, I will," Emmett said, bursting through the door with yet another armful of wood. He seemed to be making a habit of interrupting me this morning. After setting the wood down in a pile, he leaned close to Martha and, in a loud whisper, said, "Throw in some extry ham and taters for breakfast, ma'am, and you won't have to ask Wash a-tall."

With a straight face, Martha looked at the old sergeant and said, "Mr. Emmett, you are a scamp. But then so was my mister. I'll throw in the extra ham and potatoes for all that firewood you brought in. Should last me a day or so."

"Anytime, ma'am. Anytime," Emmett said with that same broad smile and poured the both of us more coffee.

Riley made an appearance in another ten minutes and we got him a cup of coffee too. Some other gent dressed in traveling broadcloth made his way downstairs but I figured he could wait a few more minutes as the three of us moved out to the community table not far from the kitchen door.

Martha must have sliced some onion and fried it with the potatoes for they had a different taste to them when she served us, one I didn't mind at all. Real inventive, this woman.

True to her word, the meal consisted of ham, flannel cakes, fried potatoes, and biscuits and honey. And it all tasted mighty fine. Martha also made sure that Emmett got his second serving of ham and potatoes, just as she'd promised. The portions of each that she served up were big enough for me to be satisfied with the one serving I had. I reckon there are times when taste makes up for bulk.

"Well, what do you think, Wash?" Martha asked when all of us were done and she was clearing the table. At first I gave her a quizzical glance, not sure what she was talking about. Then she said, "You know, taking Maria to the church service this morning. I'd consider it a personal favor if you would."

I finished what was left in my coffee cup, I reckon just to have something to do while I mulled over her proposition in my mind. Then I shrugged. What the hell. It couldn't hurt to do nothing more than walk the woman to church, could it? What was so bad about that?

"All right, Miss Martha, I'll do it," I said, "but only for you."

She gave my arm a gentle squeeze and smiled at me. "Thanks, Wash. I owe you one."

I was about to leave but stopped. Martha was walking away when I grabbed her by her own elbow and swung her around to face me. The whole thing caught her by surprise, but what astonished her most was when I leaned down and kissed her on the cheek.

"Don't sell yourself short, Martha," I said, looking right into her eyes as I spoke. "You ask me, you're a far piece from being old. Yes, ma'am, a far piece."

I had a notion she hadn't heard words like that in years, for they did a lot to that smile on her face. Even added a bit of blush that only Mother Nature can give a body.

"Well, thank you, Wash. Thank you very much," she said as she regained her composure. "That'll get you an extra drumstick at the table this afternoon. You know that, don't you?" Her smile was as big and broad as Emmett's as she turned to go.

"I'll count on it," I said as I headed for the door.

Truth to tell, I felt pretty good as I left Ma Stoner's that morning. Hell, everyone needs to be told they're doing a good job once in a while. And Martha, well, I reckon I figured her time had come.

CHAPTER
★ 20 ★

If the prisoner, Richards, did indeed have a leg broken in two places, Martha was right. It would be damned hard for him to get around in that cell, much less try to stage some kind of break from jail, which is what the local law was implying. How in the hell could a man with a broken leg be dangerous, especially when he is incarcerated in the local jail? Of course, the only way I could really find out who was telling the truth would be to head out to boot hill in the middle of the night and dig up Richards's grave and examine his legs for myself. But aside from the fact that digging a grave up would make me look like some kind of grave robber, the thought of giving up a good night's sleep didn't appeal to me either. Pondering over who was telling the truth in Sendero and who wasn't got to be right heavy on my mind as I walked toward Annie's Place. I hardly noticed that Emmett and Riley were right behind me all the way to the cafe.

"Morning, boys," Maria said with a smile as we entered the eatery. To which we all doffed our hats and replied in kind. "Satisfied as you all look, I reckon you had breakfast at Martha's this morning." She paused a moment as we took up seats at a table, then looked at me as though doing a study of me. "You, on the other hand, look like you've got something bothering you."

I shrugged noncommittally. "Just something I've been toying with that I can't get out of my mind," I admitted.

"Anything I can help you with?" she asked, going into that playful mood of hers again. I don't reckon she had forgotten last night's episode either.

"No, ma'am, nothing at the moment I can think of," I replied, feeling a slow red creeping sensation at the bottom of my neck and hoping my two friends didn't get overly curious about it.

"There is something he has to ask you, though," Riley said with an impish grin of his own. I suddenly found myself wondering why everyone was so fine and dandy feeling this morning. Or was that something this newfangled holiday was supposed to do to a body? As grandma once put it, go figure.

"Oh?" Maria was about to leave to get the three of us coffee but stopped and turned back to face me.

"Yes, ma'am," I said in my politest manner. "I understand you're needing an escort to the church service this morning." I'd hate to say I spit the words out, but I will admit it was a mite of a relief to have them out of me.

I wasn't all that sure the surprise this woman showed was anything more than put-on, my instinct telling me this whole scheme was something both Maria and Martha had concocted between the two of them. "Oh? Really? How nice! Why, I'm flattered that you've asked me, Mr. Carston," was what she said. But like I say, it would have made more sense to hear her speak the words on some play-actor's stage, they sounded that put-on.

Then she was gone, back in a minute with cups and the coffee to fill them with, her face looking happy as a lark. I tried not to notice that she kept staring at me out of the corner of her eye as she spent her time going about her duties as a waitress, flitting about the room here and there with some customer's order.

Emmett, Riley, and I were discussing what we'd found out about Joshua and how he'd wound up in the fix he was in, when Harry, Maria's father, approached our table. He was nowhere near as big as Big John Porter, back in Twin Rifles, running just a little taller than normal in height. But he was broad of shoulder and thick of chest, I'll give him that. And from the look of him, I gauged he'd have no trouble holding his own in a good fight. I reckon he reminded me of Chance in that way.

"I turned Maria loose for the morning," he said, addressing me in particular. "That church service is going to be held a mite earlier than they usually do around here. Seems every woman in town has got herself a pie she ain't yet baked and needs all that extra time, so the preacher is holding the service an hour earlier than usual."

"Tell me about it, brother," Emmett said with a chuckle. "Women always think they got something else to do and put a man in a hurry doing it."

"Anyway, she's gone to get fancied up for the service and all," Harry said. "Just wanted to tell you I thank you for escorting my Maria. She's a fine young lady."

"I'm sure she is," I replied in a respectful tone. "And it's my pleasure to take her to church."

I could see by the twinkle in his eye that he was real proud of Maria, likely just for being his daughter. Of course, as long as a woman could stay out of the red-light districts of a town, why, she could likely lead a respectable life.

"Say, why don't I dish up you boys a piece of pie to go along with that coffee?" he asked of a sudden. "It's gonna be a couple three hours or so once those women get to baking them pies afore they lay out today's spread, you know."

"Well, now, that's right neighborly," Riley said. I noticed he was acting a mite friendlier than he had been. Maybe the lad had actually done some serious thinking about his future, as I'd suggested to him.

"Besides," Harry said when he returned with three pieces of pumpkin pie, "you know how long it takes a woman to get ready for anything."

We all nodded agreement and he left with our thanks.

It was going on half-past nine when Maria showed up in her Sunday-go-to-meeting dress. It was right dressy, with frills and petticoats galore. Why, it even looked respectable, which made it good enough to go to church in, I reckon. The service was supposed to start at ten o'clock, she said, so we left right away to get a seat at the church.

I don't know why it is, but some men on this frontier you can near judge by their size. Every salesman I've seen runs to short and squat in size. And I don't believe I've seen a preacher yet who wasn't as long in the leg as he was with his sermons. Lawmen seemed to run any variation of sizes in between. The Reverend Appleby was a tall, gaunt-looking sort who would have trouble making a lap even when he sat. His Adam's apple bobbed up and down even when he wasn't talking, which didn't seem to be often. Or maybe that was just the fact that he was catching up on old times with the local women.

"Dear me," he said in a soft voice about ten minutes before the service was to begin.

"What's the matter, padre?" Riley asked. Riley, Emmett, and me were about the only men congregated at this church meeting, other than the preacher himself. "Lose something, did you?"

"Why, I believe I have." The man was looking about taking in the whole crowd outside the church. When he had everyone's attention, he said, "Pardon me, ladies, but surely you're not all single women. Not with such beauty among you." When several of the women blushed, he said, "Then where are your husbands, dear women? Are they not of your faith, is that it?"

"I hate to admit it, reverend, but mine is sitting over at the Avalon Saloon," one woman said, all sense of beauty now gone from her face. It was filled instead with a mixture of shame and frustration.

138

Pretty soon a whole lot of these women were admitting to the same thing. Their men had decided to play some poker and have a few drinks at the Avalon while they did the praying for the family.

"But prayer is for everyone, my dear women," Reverend Appleby said, apparently astonished that anyone could think otherwise.

"Damn right, padre!" Riley said, suddenly explosive and surprising us all with his language, especially considering that he was speaking to a man of the cloth and most of the women in town.

"I beg your pardon, sir?" the good reverend said, as surprised as the women surrounding him.

"Don't go begging for nothing, padre," Riley said, his voice full of authority. I found myself wondering if he hadn't held such a position like this at sometime in his past, for it sure did come easy to the young lad. "Don't beg for nothing. You just escort these young ladies into your holy place there and get 'em seated and open up your Good Book. I'll be back in two shakes."

"But where are you going, young man?" Appleby said in a confused voice as Riley began walking off.

Riley stopped, spun around to face the preacher. "Why, I'm getting their men! It's what you're needing, ain't it?"

"Yes," the reverend said in a soft voice, filled with amazement as he watched Riley go about his business.

Over his shoulder, Riley yelled to Emmett and me, "Well, are you coming along or not? I can't do this alone, you know."

Emmett and I looked at one another. I raised my eyebrows. Emmett shrugged, admitting to just as much confusion as the rest of us, I reckon. We followed Riley, who'd taken off at a good quick pace.

"After all, he can't do this alone," Emmett said.

"Nope. Sure can't."

"I wonder if he knows he could get himself killed doing this," Emmett said when we were halfway to the saloon. "I've known more than one man who'd kill you over trying to break up his poker game or his drinking. Hell, I'm one of them!"

But Riley had a mind of his own, it seemed. He charged through the batwing doors, the two of us right behind him. And as he entered the Avalon, he pulled his six-gun and fired it into the air.

"Got your attention, did I, gents?" he said in a voice loud enough for all to hear.

"What the hell do you want?" an angry bartender growled, moving his hand down underneath the bar as he spoke.

Emmett pulled his Colt pistol and leveled it at the bartender. "You don't want to do that, pilgrim. It could be downright unhealthful if you come up with anything but an empty hand." The bartender didn't have to ask what he was talking about. From the look about him, I figured he'd been called like this before, and the only reason he was still alive was because he'd come up with an empty hand.

"Listen up, you men," Riley said, still holding well to that commanding voice of his. "Your wives are down at the church and feeling almighty embarrassed because you fools ain't there with 'em. Well, you're gonna be! I hear tell this is a day to give thanks, and you men are gonna do it right alongside your wives. Now, come on!" With that he waved his pistol at the lot of them, most of whom had taken seats at tables where a deck of cards was handy.

"Riley, you put that damned gun away and stop acting like a drunk or I'll put you away," Randall Waite said, stepping away from the bar.

I took a step toward Waite and pulled my Colt Conversion model and stuck it in his face.

"You know, *deputy*," I said, snarling the last word as though it were a degrading one, and on Waite it was, "you don't impress me at all. Now, I ain't killed anyone yet with this brand-new pistol of my brother's, so if you feel like getting froggy, why, you just leap." If my words didn't stop the man, the look of this six-gun in my hand must have, for Randall Waite had nothing to say. Nothing at all.

Riley's words and actions seemed to have shocked all of the husbands who had left their wives for a game of cards and he soon had every man jack of them marching out the door like any number of sergeants I'd seen in the war.

I think any of those women—maybe even the reverend himself—who doubted the fact that miracles happen every once in a while, well, they were true believers when they saw their husbands marching into that church, hat in hand and taking up a seat right next to them. All in silence too.

Riley was standing in the back of the church with Emmett and me as the preacher began his service, when one of the older women in town approached him.

"Young man, I have always thought of you as little more than a bully and a ruffian," she said to him in a stern but soft voice. After but a moment's pause, she added, "I may have been wrong."

141

"Yes, ma'am," Riley said in his own soft humble tone. "Thank you, ma'am."

A brief smile cracked the woman's thin lips. "You make sure and join us at that turkey dinner meal this afternoon. I think we'd all be proud to have you." Then she was seated again, gone as quickly as she had appeared.

"Now, would you believe that?" Emmett said in what I took to be a bit of amazement. I reckon he was as surprised as I was.

Riley had a crooked grin on his face as he said, "Well, I had to get an invite to that shindig somehow."

Maybe. But something told me that there was more to what Riley had done than a simple invitation to a turkey dinner.

A lot more.

CHAPTER
★ 21 ★

Reverend Appleby's sermon was about what you'd expect for the occasion, I reckon. Love thy neighbor and be thankful for what you have on this earth, little as it might be. Somewhere along the way, he fit in God's hand—how we all had what we had and how we should all be thankful for the Almighty looking over us the way He does. I reckon if you're real religious, like most women in this world are brought up to be, you'll pack a heap of belief in that line of thought. But a man sees a lot more of the world than most women do, I think, and it's been my experience that if a man is to stay alive . . . well, it ain't that he's got to disbelieve in the Maker so much as it is having a more practical belief in his own abilities to survive.

143

I could recall a comment old Charlie Goodnight made on that trail drive me and Chance were on a year back. Someone had made note of that beatitude, or whatever it was, the one about the meek inheriting the earth. Uncle Charlie, why, he had his own vision of just how far the meek would get on this frontier. "The meek ain't gonna inherit nothing west of St. Louis." He'd scowled to the man, and we all laughed a mite. Of course, if you thought about it, Uncle Charlie was probably right by no stretch of the imagination.

"I want to thank you men for helping gather up the menfolk of this town, shall we say?" the good preacher said to Riley, Emmett, and me when the services were over and folks were filing out of church. "I've always thought that couples should be attuned to religion as one, don't you agree?"

"Oh, yes sir, padre," Riley said with a note of firm conviction and a nod of the head.

"You bet, reverend," Emmett agreed heartily. If I knew Emmett, he was subscribing to everything the man said more so he wouldn't have to discuss anything else of a religious nature, as opposed to wanting to stick around and discuss what exactly Jesus and the last supper had to do with the Pilgrims and Thanksgiving. If you know what I mean.

"And you, sir?" the reverend asked of me when I hadn't jumped right up and shook his hand over the matter.

"If you say so, reverend," I replied with a mite of a shrug. "I reckon that's more your area than mine."

"Excuse me, Reverend Appleby," Maria said when everyone was nearly filed out of the church and gone. "I hate to cut this conversation short, but I need Wash to escort me back to the cafe so I can help Pa with those pies and the dinner meal."

"Certainly." The preacher smiled as Maria hooked her arm through mine and led me off from the group. I didn't say anything but I got to wondering who was leading who as we walked to Annie's Place.

"It was a nice service, don't you think?" she asked halfway to the cafe.

"I reckon. I never was big on churchgoing."

She smiled at my remark and was silent the rest of the way. It was when we got to the cafe that she surprised me again. Like any gentleman, I'd been walking on the outside of the lady as we strolled along, which put her right next to the windows and buildings and such. It also put her closest to the alley next to the cafe when we came to it. She quick stepped into it, then yanked my arm, pulling me toward her into the alley too. My instinct told me to go for my gun but before I could yank it out she stood before me and was kissing me again.

"You're gonna have to stop this, Maria," I said, pushing her away from me at arm's length. Not that I kissed her back or anything, you understand. Not on your life! But in all honesty I'd have to admit that I didn't pull myself away from her as quickly as I likely should have either.

"I really scare you, don't I?" she said, a cunning smile coming to her face now. Her mind was working as she spoke, that much I knew for sure. I'd also decided she was one woman who set her cap and went after whatever was in her sights. And me, I was wanting to get out of her sight as soon as possible.

"No, Maria, it ain't that. It ain't that at all." My

145

hands dropped to my sides and I tried to fix a determined look upon my face, although I'd be the first to admit it wasn't an easy thing to do. "Damn it, woman, I'm married, just like I told you. Now I don't want you kissing me or doing any other kind of tomfoolery around me, you understand?" By the time I got the words out, my determination had changed to anger and I think she saw that. Still, it didn't stop her from having her way.

"Sure, Mr. Carston, anything you say. I'll keep in mind that you're a married man, especially when I serve your table." She said it cold as fish on ice. Then she turned to go, but if the ominous look on her face was any indication, I wasn't sure she believed—or understood—a damn thing I'd said.

Not a thing.

Something told me that it wouldn't be long before things came to a head in Sendero concerning Joshua and whatever it was that had gotten him put in jail. I'll grant you, the day had started out with a good feeling. But when Maria had yanked me into the alley the way she just did, why, I had a notion the day wouldn't be all that good after all. It was nothing more than a gut feeling, the kind you get when you can't prove something but you just *know* that what you're feeling is true.

It crossed my mind that I might as well pay a visit to the livery stable and see if the old man I'd encountered when I first put up my horse was still taking care of him. Hell, for all I knew, he might have raised the rates overnight, which would mean I owed him a couple nights worth of feed and grain. And that fellow was just mean enough to send the vigilantes out after me to collect his money.

The old man wasn't there when I arrived at the livery, so I took the liberty of checking on my mount, making sure he'd been taken care of properly. From all indications he had been, likely living as well or better than I had been. I checked my saddle, which was still all in order.

"Find anything missing?" a voice behind me said. Once again I found myself going for my gun, stopping only when my hand had engulfed the pistol grip.

"No. It's fine," I said as I turned around to face him. I still hadn't let my hand drop away from the six-gun in my holster though.

"Touchy bird, ain't ye?" His face screwed up into a frown that said he didn't like youngsters like me talking back to him the way I was.

"Some would say so, I reckon."

"While you're here, you can pay me a mite more for taking care of that mount of yours," he said. "That is if you ain't run out of money yet."

If his words were meant to bring out the mad in me, I reckon he was coming close. I fished around in my pocket until I found the coin I was looking for and plunked it in his hand. "This oughtta hold you another day or two."

"And a good day to you too," he said in his best sarcastic tone and wandered off to pitch some hay, which was presumably more important than socializing with me.

I was walking out of the livery when something struck me as odd and I backed up a mite. I counted all of the stalls and sure enough, it looked like the same amount of horses were in the stalls as had been there the day I first rode into town.

"Say, friend, would you tell me something?" I asked, walking up behind him but making sure I was a safe distance away from him, a distance far enough away so he couldn't accidentally stick that three-pronged tool into some part of me.

"If I can. But make it quick, I've got work to do."

"Sure," I said and asked him if he'd gotten any new horses to put up since I'd come into town.

"Nope." He shook his head, as though giving serious thought to the subject. "Onliest one come into town since you is that preacher fella, and he keeps his hoss in a small barn back of the church." He grumbled to himself and said, "Couldn't afford to pay me to keep his hoss anyway." Which was all too true, for most circuit riding preachers didn't make a whole lot of money at the profession. Mostly, they relied on the charity of the people in the community they were passing through to provide them food and shelter and a place to sleep.

"None come in and none left, is that it?" I asked in a curious manner.

"That's right, son," he said and went back to pitching his hay.

"Son of a bitch," I said, mumbling the words to myself as I walked off, leaving the old man to himself. But over my shoulder I could see I'd made him curious by my oath.

Somehow I knew it had happened that way. I knew it!

"Say, deputy marshal," a man called to me as I passed the telegraph office. I was heading for Ma

Stoner's boardinghouse, figuring I might meet Riley and Emmett back there, when I had passed the telegraph office.

"What is it, friend?"

"I got a wire for you while you were at the church services this morning," he said and handed me a sheet of paper.

It was what I'd half expected but had hoped against. Still, after seeing what I'd just seen at the livery, and then this telegraph, well, the evidence seemed to be pretty strong.

One of the things I'd done just before visiting the Avalon Saloon when first arriving in town was to hunt up the telegraph office and send a wire to Pa, asking about verifying for me the fact that he had sent me to Sendero to pick up a prisoner—and Joshua if he could be found. But I'd also told Pa to expect a rider from the marshal of Sendero requesting the same information, just as I'd told Forrest Haney to do. After all, I didn't know there was a telegraph at Sendero at the time, and was used to sending riders to ferret out information, just like Pa usually did. So it was a surprise to find out the telegraph had come to Sendero just as it had to Twin Rifles.

What was even more surprising was the wire I'd just gotten from Pa. He'd waited a couple of days but no rider from Sendero had ever showed up. Not a one, and he thought I'd like to know that. I reckon he was as suspicious as I was of what had happened. Or hadn't happened, as the case seemed to be.

Could it be that Forrest Haney never had any

intention of sending a wire to Twin Rifles to confirm what I'd told him about Joshua? From what the old man at the livery had told me, that seemed a real possibility, for not a horse had left the livery stable since I'd come to Sendero.

"Tell me something, friend," I said to the telegraph operator, a pudgy little fellow with a moon-shaped face. Before I went jumping to conclusions, I wanted to make sure I'd checked out all avenues on this matter. After all, maybe Haney had simply gotten busy and forgotten to send a rider to Twin Rifles. Then it crossed my mind that he might not have sent a rider at all, but for good reason.

"Sure. What do you want to know, deputy?"

"Your marshal use this telegraph machine of yours a lot, does he?" I asked.

The man smiled. "Oh, yes, sir. Ever since it come in six months ago, why, he makes real good use of it. Real good use of it."

"I see." I scratched my jaw, running a thought through my mind. I was going to give the man one last chance, one last benefit of the doubt. "You recall as he used it over the last couple of days?"

"No, not right off hand," he replied. "But here, let me check," he added and pulled out his logbook and set to checking the last few days worth of entries. "Nope. Not since last week, he ain't used it."

"Thanks."

I folded the wire and put it in my shirt pocket, all of a sudden remembering how cold it was outside. Or was that a chill I felt running down my spine? A chill that had nothing to do with the temperature.

"Son of a bitch," I mumbled to myself again as I left the telegraph office. Just like the old man at the livery stable, I suddenly had the telegrapher's curious attention.

I felt the mad build in me as I left, knowing full well that Marshal Forrest Haney had never intended to send a rider or a wire to Twin Rifles.

Never!

CHAPTER

★ 22 ★

The door almost came unhinged as I flung it open, bouncing off the wall and coming back at me. It rebounded off my arm on the backswing, but I can't recall even noticing the pain if there was any. I was that mad.

I stood there a minute, looking over the marshal's office, my eyes winding up on Forrest Haney, who looked real unsettled at the moment.

"What's the matter, marshal, never been surprised like that before?" I said with a growl. I didn't need any help sounding mean and insulting. Hell, neither would you if you were as mad as I was.

"Now what the hell's this all about?" Haney asked, rising from his desk. It was plain to see that he hadn't been in this kind of position for this long by simply sitting on his ass. By the time he rounded the corner of his desk he was looking as mad as I was feeling. Which suited me just fine.

We were both taking a step or two toward one another when I hit him. And I mean hard. Right on the jaw. It was the same kind of force I recalled using on Chance when the two of us had tangled in the past. And, just like my brother, this man was big enough to take a good hard punch. He staggered to the rear a mite, which was all the time I needed to poke a left jab at the other side of his face and hit him again with a solid hard right. It was enough to knock him ass over teakettle and leave him sprawled out on the floor, just like I'd done to Riley when I'd first met him.

"Good for you, Wash! Good for you!" I heard Joshua yell across the room from his cell. I gave him a quick glance and saw the ear-to-ear grin on his face. But no sooner did I catch sight of it than the look turned to one of fear.

He was saying "Look out!" when I pulled Chance's Colt Conversion out and had it pointed right at Forrest Haney, his own hand still on the grip of his holstered six-gun.

"Go ahead, Haney," I said, a growl still stuck in my throat as I spoke. It was a mite colder now though and he knew I meant business. "As soon as that pistol clears leather, you're a dead man. Guaranteed." The fear had gone from Joshua's eyes to those of Forrest Haney, and it wasn't a pretty sight. I reckon he knew he could lose face and never have my respect or die trying to live up to the code—whatever it was—he lived by. He tried something different.

"You want to tell me just what it is that set you off,

son?" he asked, slowly getting to his feet. He rubbed his jaw and tried moving it about some to see if it had been damaged any more than it must have felt. Then he made his way to his desk and took his seat behind it, exactly where I'd found him when I'd barged in.

"You didn't send a man to Twin Rifles like I suggested, did you?"

"Well, I—"

"You didn't send a wire on that new telegraph of yours either," I said in an accusing tone. "I know. I checked the livery stable and the telegraph office. You know what that makes you, Haney?"

"No, but I imagine I'm gonna hear your version of it, whether I like it or not," he said, still rubbing his jaw in a tender manner.

"It makes you a goddamn liar," I said between gritted teeth. My look wasn't any friendlier than my words.

"I hope that preacher don't hear you talk like that." I didn't know whether he was stalling for time or being the smart aleck that he seemed to be at times. Nor did I care.

"Shut up, Haney." I holstered my Colt, feeling mad enough to know within me that I could tear this man apart if I had to and not even work up a sweat over it. I glared into his eyes as I said, "You killed that Richards fella, didn't you? I can't prove it, but instinct tells me you killed the man for one reason or another. Then you pinned it all on Joshua there, likely because he was handy and nothing else."

"You've got all the questions and all the answers, don't you, Carston?" he said, suddenly regaining any confidence he might have lost. "The trouble with you, kid, is you ain't sure which questions match up with which answers."

"That ain't it at all, marshal, and you know it," Joshua said in an angry tone. "He just ain't got it all figgered out yet, is all. But don't you worry, lawman, ole Wash, he's a right smart man and he'll find out what it is you're a-hiding. Sure enough, he will."

Forrest Haney had apparently had enough of being ordered around in his own domain. With a stern voice he said over his shoulder, "You shut your trap, hill man." Then, to me, he frowned and said, "As for you, you lay another hand on me and I'll bury you the same day."

I backed up toward the door, not sure I could trust this man not to back shoot me on my way out. After all, I had taken a fist to him. And those were none too friendly as far as terms go between two men. So I eased my way toward the door, back first.

"I don't know where you started out, Haney, but I'd bet a dollar that it was a far piece from where you wound up," I said in an even tone.

"Oh? Getting philosophical now, are you?" he said, still holding his own.

"No, not philosophical at all, Haney. Just telling the truth, something you likely ain't heard in some time." I wasn't sure if what was crossing my mind were the right words, but I knew the feeling was right. I also knew that like it or not, Marshal Forrest Haney needed to hear those words. "Maybe at one time you were a good man, Haney, but I've got a notion—as much as a man can gather over a two-day period— that sometime not too long ago you gave up the law as it's supposed to be practiced."

I opened the door, ready to leave, and finished what I thought needed saying. "Seeing a man like you wearing a badge like that, well, it purely makes me sick." I spat on his floor, not really caring what he might think of the gesture.

Then I was gone.

If anyone else had said those words, they might not have meant a thing to the man, for that was part of being a lawman. You learned to take the good compliments with the bad and let the bad ones roll off your back, like water off a duck. But the words Forrest Haney had just heard had come from another lawman.

Maybe they would make a difference.

CHAPTER
★ 23 ★

Martha Stoner was busy as could be in her kitchen, rushing from one part of it to another, tending to everything from pies to meats to any number of fancified dishes that would be served with the turkeys and other main courses.

"Am I busy, you ask?" she said in a somewhat harried voice when I inquired as to what she was doing. "Of course I'm not busy. I wish I had more things to do, more to take care of for this meal. Of course I'm not busy!"

"I don't suppose you can use any help, can you?" If nothing else, I figured I'd better ask out of politeness; no use in standing there like a fool when this woman was working as hard as she was.

"You're two hours late, son," was her reply. Haughty was how her voice sounded now. Me, I didn't say a word. Not a one. Then, after a moments silence, she looked at me and said, "Which direction are you going? I know you aren't just staying around here to smell the food."

"No, ma'am. Actually, I was wondering if you'd seen my friends, Emmett and Riley. Thought they might have dropped by here after the church service." If I sounded extra polite it was because this was the woman who would likely be responsible for a good share of the food that would be served this afternoon. And I didn't want to get on her bad side, for what she had cooked up so far smelled right tasty. Pies and biscuits and all those condiments getting cooked up like they were . . .

"Oh, sure," she said with a nod. "Left here about half an hour ago. Sent 'em down to the church with an armful of deadwood apiece. Reverend Appleby promised me he'd have that potbellied stove going so we could set out some of this food and keep it relatively warm until mealtime." She gave herself a brief hug and added with a smile, "One of the joys of working in a kitchen in weather like this, I suppose."

"I won't fault you there, Martha, not one bit," I said, returning her smile.

"Here," she said and out of nowhere produced an oblong flat tray, set it on a table and began placing as many pies as she could on it. "See if you can't manage to carry this down to the church without spilling them all over the place. You'll find your friends down there, I suspect."

"Yes, ma'am," I said, ready to obey her orders. Had to stay on her good side, remember? I was about to pick up the tray when a thought struck me. "Say, Miss Martha, are you sure you'll have enough firewood for tomorrow after you get through with all of this cooking today?"

But Martha Stoner had a handle on everything, as always. "I'm not even worried about it, young man."

"Oh?"

Her smile had a seductive look about it as she said, "I'll just offer that big cavalryman another slice of meat for his plate when he wanders back here tomorrow morning." Yes sir, Martha Stoner had a handle on it all.

I was about to pick up the tray again when she said, "I hope you and Maria got along well, escorting her to church and all." I thought I detected a hint of curiosity in her words.

"Actually, Martha, I had to explain to her that I really am a married man and don't care to have her kissing me like she's done the last couple of days. My wife would kill her and me if she ever found out about that, and Sarah Ann's not a jealous woman by any means," I said.

"She just don't want to share her man with anyone, is that it?" she said.

"I reckon you could say that. Took that wedding vow for every word in it. Got real serious about it, she did."

"I can understand that," Martha said with a nod. "My mister was like that too." She sighed and added, "Oh, well, Maria will find a man one of these days."

"Yeah."

Then as I picked up the tray of pies, she opened the door for me and I made my way down to the church.

"And if you eat so much as a crumb on that tray,

you'll never eat at my table again!" she yelled after me from the doorway of her boardinghouse.

"Don't recall seeing this many people gather for a meal since my days in the cavalry," Emmett said with an astonished look. The good reverend did indeed have that potbellied stove fired up. And the church, otherwise an empty shell if I guessed right, was now filling to capacity with the men and women of the community.

"Know just what you mean, hoss," I said, knowing full well exactly what Emmett was talking about. I recalled my days with Terry's Texas Rangers and how we'd all huddle around a fire when the winter months came, using the blazing flames as much to warm our bodies as we did to heat our food. "The only difference was that we didn't do one hell of a lot of jabbering back then." All about us friends and neighbors were talking among themselves as though they hadn't seen one another in some time.

Emmett nodded in silence. "The presence of death does things like that to a man. Does it to all men in those circumstances, I reckon."

Except for occasional fits of coughing, Riley was silent throughout our conversation, likely too young to have experienced the kind of warfare that Emmett and I were talking about. Still, he took it all in with an interest I hadn't seen in him before. Maybe the boy was finding the kind of friends he needed to get through this ordeal called consumption.

"Wish I'd been there," he finally said in a yearning voice that meant exactly what the words said.

"No you don't, sonny," Emmett said in an equally emphatic tone. "No you don't. Believe me, the only thing a man wants to remember about going through a war is the stories he can tell his grandchildren."

"And if he's lucky, he'll do it when he's old and gray," I added to Emmett's words. "When the hurt and the pain have worn off his soul enough so he can tell those stories without breaking down and crying."

Emmett nodded agreement, but I had a notion that, like most youngsters Riley's age, war and combat would remain some kind of romantic idea that would only be diminished by the smell of smoke and the sounds of battle. The smells and sounds that made up what Emmett and Chance and me knew all too well as death.

The sun had come out and it actually seemed to warm the area, or at least I got that impression as I'd carried the pies down to the church. Maybe it was simply the heat I was feeling from those just-baked pies that had added a certain warmth to my body. Whether it was the pies or the heat from Old Sol or the gathering of the friendly people of Sendero, I'd felt a desire to be friendly to them in return. I could only hope that such a feeling would last the rest of the day. Still, in the bottom of my stomach was an ill-at-ease foreboding that told me such camaraderie was not to be. Not for me, anyway.

Several wagons pulled up and were soon dispatched of their loads, which were the community tables we'd be eating our meals from in a short time. Riley and Emmett disappeared for a while and Maria and her father, Harry, showed up with a small entourage and plenty more food to be laid out on the community tables.

"Can I give you a hand?" I asked the father and daughter, although in all honesty I had addressed myself to Harry. Maria might still be in a spiteful mood.

Harry invited me to help him set up more tables, while Maria and several other women set individual settings and plates. When the meal was ready to be served, I stood next to Maria and helped her dish out servings of dressing and potatoes and candied yams to the people as they walked by.

"You aren't holding a grudge against me, are you?" I asked when the line eased up some.

I don't know whether the look about her was put-on or for real, but I was hoping it was sincere when she turned to me and gave me a brief smile. "No, I'm not holding a grudge. Daddy taught me not to behave like that."

"Good." I spooned out more food before there was another letup in the line. "I like you and all, Maria, but I'm afraid I just ain't got much of a romantic interest in you."

My words brought tears to her eyes and I handed her my kerchief, which she dabbed at the side of her eyes. I felt embarrassed as all get-out and knew I had to explain myself. "I reckon I never was much good with words to a woman. Never did get that good with Sarah Ann either."

"I imagine she's quite pretty," Maria said when the crying stopped.

"Yes, ma'am," I answered with a good deal of pride. "Prettiest woman I ever did lay eyes upon. Yes, ma'am."

The conversation dried up then about as quick as a brief shower at high noon in July in the Mojave Desert. We spent upward of half an hour filling people's plates with food and holding polite conversation with them. But between us, well, I reckon all the words had been said. All that could be said without doing any more damage, that is.

After everyone else had been fed, I filled my own plate with what was left, which seemed to be a goodly amount from the look of it. And true to her word, Martha Stoner had saved me a drumstick and a thigh. Along with a good hot cup of coffee, it all tasted as though it were worth waiting for. I was halfway through my drumstick when Riley set his git-up end down next to me. Along with him, he'd brought a fairly large piece of mincemeat pie and a cup of coffee.

"Mighty good feed, wouldn't you say?" were his first words.

"Ain't seen a spread like this in some time," was my reply between mouthfuls of food.

He ate about half of his pie in silence before turning to me and saying, "Say, Wash, are you still interested in that Richards fella? The one that friend of yours is supposed to have killed?"

I nodded, any complacency I might have been feeling suddenly replaced by a desire to hear what this man had to say. After all, my main reason for coming to Sendero had been to find Joshua and that prisoner.

"You see that feller over yonder?" he asked and nodded his head toward a man in a black suit. "The one that's near as reedy as the reverend."

"Yeah," I said around more turkey.

"I was just talking to him. Undertaker, don't you know. Does carpentry work on the side," he said. "Made sure and get that all out to me before I'd even shook his hand."

"Is this your roundabout way of telling me something, Riley?" I said, a mite impatiently I'll admit.

163

"'Cause if it is, you're taking longer than need be to do it."

"You know that your man Richards had him a couple of breaks in his leg," he asked, "enough to keep him from doing any walking of any kind?"

"Yeah." I nodded. "Heard about that last night." Not that I was wanting to belittle the lad, you understand. Hell, he could have heard Maria tell me that in my doorway, as paper-thin as the walls to our rooms were. And who was to say this lad wasn't just trying to make himself sound important? After seeing Riley be as full of himself as he could be when I'd first met him, it wouldn't be out of the question now. Besides, as down-and-out as he'd been feeling, he likely could use a lift of his spirits, and passing on important information to me about the case I was investigating could do just that.

"Then tell me, this, lawman," he said, a note of arrogance creeping into his voice now. "Do you know how the man was killed?"

I shrugged. "Shot, wasn't he?"

"Yeah, but where?" That was the rub, the important piece of information that Riley had found out.

I shook my head, suddenly wanting to know what knowledge Riley had about this killing, no matter what his voice might sound like. "Where?"

"In the back." He said the words very hard, very deliberately, as though he knew the importance of each one. And he was right, for this put a whole new light on things.

I stopped shoveling food into my mouth long enough to chew what I had and say, "Are you sure?"

"Mr. Undertaker there told me so. I figure a man in that profession ought to know what he's talking about," he said with a good deal of pride. He must have seen the realization of what this all meant in my eyes, for he smiled and said, "Puts a mighty different twist on things, don't it?"

"I'll say." And that it did. I'd never really questioned Haney or anyone else on how Richards had died. All either of them had said was that the man had been killed while trying to escape, which, when I thought of it, sounded real fishy to begin with. I ate the rest of my food slowly, chewing each bite and savoring the taste. But young Riley must have seen that, with all that chewing going on, my mind was working too.

How could I have been so stupid? How could I have overlooked the obvious? Pa would never have done that. He would have seen it right off and done something about it. Which showed you how much of a professional lawman I was.

"Makes you mad, don't it?" Riley said after holding his cup up for more coffee as one of the women with a coffeepot passed us by.

"Madder than hell."

I had Joshua's story on how it was he came to be put in jail, a story I would believe far more easily than I would that of Waite or Haney. Besides—and here was what bothered me—Joshua had supposedly been arrested for killing the prisoner. That might make some kind of sense if Haney hadn't told me that Richards had been killed while trying to escape. That didn't make sense at all. Why would Joshua, a deputy marshal—a federal lawman at that—be jailed for having shot a prisoner while trying to escape? He wouldn't have, even I knew that.

But based on what Riley had just told me, I knew it couldn't have been Joshua who'd done the killing.

Joshua wasn't a back shooter, of that I was certain. The man came from the hills back east somewhere and if I knew anything about those people, I knew that they had a more than strict code of ethics, and back shooting wasn't a part of it. Not at all. So that left either Randall Waite or Forrest Haney, and I would have bet every last penny I had on either of the two. Or, maybe both in a conspiracy.

"What are you thinking, Wash?" Riley asked, suddenly acting as though he were my saddle pard from way back.

"Have 'em save me a piece of pie, Riley," I said as I pushed myself away from the community table. "I ain't through hunting yet."

It took a while to find him, but I did. I had to walk about the crowds of townspeople both sitting and standing, looking for Marshal Haney. By the time I spotted him, he was heading behind the church. At the time I was determined to get him off to one side and talk to him about what I considered to be false arrest charges for starters. But by the time I was close to rounding the back side of that church building, I was too late. Forrest Haney was already in conversation with someone else. I leaned back against the church wall, listening to what the two had to say.

". . . and I say you'll keep your mouth shut," the man said in a sour voice. Madder than hell, from the sound of him. And a voice that was awfully familiar.

"The hell you will," Haney growled right back at the man. "I'm the one who runs this town, not you."

"Well, get used to not running it, *marshal.*" The last word was said as though spit out in hatred.

"Don't threaten me, sonny," the older lawman said to the man now.

"Marshal, if you don't do what I tell you, I'll go to the mayor with this whole thing. Tell him how you were in on this bank robbery gang from the start."

Then the words stopped and the man Haney had been speaking to stomped off in the other direction. Me, I turned my back to them and headed back toward the crowd, hoping I'd blend in and not be spotted by either of them.

Actually, the man Haney had been conversing with was no stranger to me at all. I didn't even have to see him stalking off to know who he was.

I was certain the voice belonged to Randall Waite.

CHAPTER
★ 24 ★

Thanksgiving Day in Twin Rifles turned out to be a real eye-opener. As in Sendero, arrangements had been made to hold early services in the town church, the only difference being the people in Twin Rifles had a permanent pastor for their church. His name was Peter Cromwell and he stood in the doorway, shaking hands and wishing well to all of his flock.

"That's a mighty pretty lady you've got on your arm, marshal," he said to Will Carston, who had been escorting Sarah Ann to the Sunday services ever since Wash had been sent to Sendero to ferret out Joshua.

"Prettiest lady we've had in our family since Cora as I recall," Will said with a proud smile as he looked down at a blushing Sarah Ann. All three of them knew that he meant every word he said. They also knew that there were times Will Carston truly missed his now-deceased wife. In fact, if it hadn't been for Margaret Ferris paying as much attention to him as she did, Will might have gone round the bend a long time ago.

"I really appreciate you holding your service this early in the morning, Reverend Cromwell," Sarah Ann said in a sincere tone. "You know how it is with the holiday and all. Papa and me will likely be cooking right up to the time we serve the dinner meal."

"Nonsense, my dear," the reverend said, taking Sarah Ann's hand in his own. "I'm delighted you saw fit to invite me. In fact, I dare say the hardest work I'll have to do will be blessing the meal and those of us fortunate enough to feast at it."

"I'm just sorry Wash ain't here for it," Will said. "I don't know how he's spending today, but he oughtta be back here in Twin Rifles come day after tomorrow, ary my figuring is correct."

"Oh, yes," the man of the cloth said, as though remembering that Will's youngest son was gone. "I'll say an extra prayer that he's bringing back Joshua with him."

"You do that, reverend," Will said before moving on to take a seat. "I figure the both of 'em are likely needing it."

Reverend Cromwell didn't have to ask where Chance was. If there was work to be done around the time a religious service was about to be held, Chance could suddenly find it to do. The reverend could count on the fingers of one hand the number of times he'd recalled seeing Will Carston's oldest boy in one of the

169

pews in this church. That didn't speak well for a man who was as free with the Lord's name—especially taking it in vain—as Chance Carston was.

Everyone had taken their seats and Reverend Cromwell had started the service when the first surprise of the day took place. The good reverend was speaking his piece when he glanced up from his book and his eyes near bulged out of his head as he looked at the rear of the church. A stir went up in the congregation and soon everyone else had taken at least one glance to the rear of the church, their eyes doing strange things in their heads too once they saw what it was the reverend had taken in.

The four Hadley Brothers had entered the church and now stood all in a row to the rear. With them was Pardee Taylor, who looked nearly as rough as the Hadleys. Or maybe it was his reputation that had given him the look. Pardee Taylor had been known for years as the town bully of Twin Rifles. He was also known to be on the road to becoming the town drunk. But then he'd changed, almost overnight. Oh, he still had a beer once in a while, but nothing as wild and woolly as before. He'd even started acting like a civilized citizen of the town proper, which had amazed many a man and nearly all of the women in town.

All five of these rough-looking men had dug up what could only presumably be called their Sunday-go-to-meeting coats and string ties. Of the five of them, the only one who really looked presentable was Pardee Taylor, but then he'd likely had more practice at it than the Hadleys. Miracle of miracles, each one of them was clean shaven.

The reverend went nervously back to reading his scripture as Will Carston got up and went back to the rear of the church.

"If you five come to start trouble, you picked the wrong day and time to do it," Will said with a low growl. It seemed that whenever he ran into the Hadleys these days, he wound up growling at them like they were untamed animals, not far from the truth by most people's standards in this town.

"Will—" Pardee started to say, but the marshal ignored him, focusing instead on the four troublemaking brothers.

"I swear to God—"

"You sure you oughtta be saying that in here, Will?" Pardee asked.

"You four heathens make any trouble for me today and I swear I'll bury you before sundown, understand?" Will Carston said, the frown on his face growing darker. To his surprise, the Hadleys didn't say a word.

"Will, they ain't making no trouble," Pardee said in a lowered voice, gently taking hold of the marshal's arm and steering him to one side. The Hadley Brothers stood stock-still, taking in Reverend Cromwell's words. "Ain't said a peep, don't you see?" When Will didn't respond, he added, "I even had 'em leave their guns up to Ernie Johnson's Saloon." Will looked toward the four brothers and each pulled back his coat to reveal no gun belts or weapons of any kind on their person. He had to shake his head and look twice at what he saw, for this wasn't like the Hadleys at all. Not at all. "Honest, Will, they'll behave. They won't make no trouble. I give you my word."

171

"It ain't even noon yet, Pardee," Will hissed at Taylor. "It's gonna be a devil of a long day for these ruffians to go without starting a fight."

"I know, Will, but they're trying. Don't that count for something?" The look on Pardee's face was near the begging stage.

The confusion Will was feeling suddenly showed in his face. Why in the hell was Pardee Taylor of all people taking such an interest in the Hadley Brothers? Why, they were all cut from the same cloth, everyone knew that. And no matter how much you cleaned up their ill-fitting suits and spruced them up, why, they'd still be the Hadley Brothers and Pardee Taylor.

"All right," Will said, shaking an impatient finger in Pardee's face. "But if they so much as disrupt my day, I'll guarantee you one thing. By God, it'll be *you* who goes to jail, Pardee, *you!*"

When the service was over, the Hadleys and Pardee Taylor stood off to one side and the congregation began to file out of the church. And if they filed out at a quicker pace than usual, it was likely because they didn't want to have anything to do with either the Hadleys or Pardee Taylor.

"I'm proud of you, boys," Reverend Cromwell said to the five black sheep when everyone else had left. "Not just that you've actually showed up at one of my services but that you were so quiet during all of it."

"Nice speechifying, preacher," Carny Hadley said as he took the reverend's hand and began to pump it.

"Yeah," Wilson Hadley said in agreement. "Ain't heard them kind of words since Aunt Priscilla read to us from the book."

When the five of them began walking back toward Ernie Johnson's Saloon—likely to pick up their guns and some hard liquor, Will thought—the reverend turned to the marshal.

"Miracles will never cease, eh, Will?" he said, watching the brothers go.

Will Carston had his eye on them too.

"The day ain't over yet, reverend," was all he'd say in reply.

It was a little after noon when Big John Porter placed the OPEN sign in his front window and began seating people for Thanksgiving dinner. Ten minutes later Chance Carston had found himself a seat. A few minutes after that, the Porter Cafe was at least half full.

"My, I'm surprised to see you here, Chance," Sarah Ann said when she came to his table. Everyone knew that Rachel had a crush on Chance, which was one reason he took most of his meals in town at the Ferris House, where Rachel Ferris lived and worked with her mother.

"Hold the pie, Sarah Ann," Chance said with a somewhat lecherous smile. "I'll be getting my desert at the Ferris House."

Sarah Ann blushed as she took his order and headed for the kitchen. She was almost to the kitchen door when she saw the Hadley Brothers and Pardee Taylor enter the Porter Cafe. But before she could say a word, Chance was at her side, ready to defend his sister-in-law. Or get into a good fight, as the case may be.

"That's far enough, boys," he said, planting both hands on his hips. "You know what Pa said about you coming in here again."

"Ain't got no guns, Chance," Carny Hadley said, pulling back his coat to show the truth of what he said.

"Come for a decent meal is all," Wilson said. "Besides," he added with a grin, "you know Ike here can't cook no better than you."

But Chance was adamant. "Don't make no difference. Pa said you wasn't to come back to Porter's Cafe and that's that." He didn't move, still standing there like a wooden Indian.

"Now wait a minute, Chance," Sarah Ann said. Her mind was obviously working as she spoke. "Are you boys serious about sitting down and eating a peaceful meal?"

"Yes, ma'am," they said in unison.

Then Sarah Ann reached over and grabbed the coffeepot she had left sitting on a nearby table. When she spoke next, it was to Carny Hadley. "No fighting? No trouble?"

The sight of the coffeepot had the effect Sarah Ann desired, especially when it was spotted by the older Hadley.

"No, ma'am," Carny said all too eagerly. "None of that, ma'am. You've got my word on it."

"That's a fact, ma'am," Wilson Hadley said, a certain amount of pride in his voice. "Ain't had a fight all day. Why, I'll tell you, Miss Sarah Ann, it's plum . . . different. Yes, ma'am."

"Then why don't you have a seat at the big table in the back, boys, and I'll be with you in a minute." You'd have thought Sarah Ann was in charge of the place, the way the five of them quietly made their way to the table and took their seats.

Chance couldn't believe what he was seeing.

Half an hour later Chance was eating his meal when a stranger came in and took a seat near the front door.

174

Chance found himself taking in this man, much as he'd seen his father do to a stranger arriving in town. He didn't look like anyone he'd seen before, nor did he seem to fit any description he'd seen on the wanted posters in Will Carston's office. Still, he kept an eye on the man as he ordered his meal.

The man was served his meal and seemed to be acting as a normal drifter would. And that was when some more of the folks of Twin Rifles got another surprise.

"Listen, sweetie, why don't you get me some coffee and be quick about it," the drifter said from across the room. When Chance looked up he saw the man had a rough grip on Sarah Ann's arm and from the look on her face he was hurting her. "I want it now," he added, giving Sarah Ann a shake when she only stood there stock-still.

Chance was pushing back his plate when a blur rushed past him and he looked up to see Carny Hadley all but running toward the stranger.

"That ain't polite at all, mister," Carny said in a mean voice as he yanked the man's hand away from Sarah Ann's arm.

"Thank you, Mr. Hadley," Sarah Ann said politely. She would have said more but Carny was in the process of pulling the man to his feet. The man, who wasn't really all that big, just thick and squat once you took in his features, took a swing at Carny with his free hand, striking Hadley across the face.

It didn't faze Carny at all. But you could tell he didn't like it. Not one bit. He brought a huge left fist up under the man, striking him in the breadbasket, nearly folding him in half from the force of the blow.

"What the hell is he doing now?" Big John Porter's voice boomed from the entry to the kitchen. "Beating up on customers?"

"No, Papa," Sarah Ann said as she stepped in front of Big John. "Believe it or not, Carny saved me from that man."

"That's a fact, John," Chance said from the side.

Meanwhile, Carny had grabbed the half-conscious man by the stack and swivel and was hauling him toward the front door. "You don't mind, do you?" he said to Big John as he steered the man toward the door.

"Spare the door," was all Big John said as he opened it for Carny. "Glass is expensive, you know."

Carny placed one hand on the man's shirt, grabbing his belt buckle and the back of his pants and literally tossed him from the premises. He rolled across the boardwalk and onto the dirt street, next to his horse.

"And don't come back!" Big John yelled after him.

Inside, Carny Hadley heard a handful of the patrons applaud his efforts. On the way back to his table he also heard a few "Well done" comments at the neighboring tables. It purely amazed him, this type of treatment.

"See, I told you it wasn't that hard to act like God-fearing people," Pardee said as though to prove a point.

"Yeah, I see what you mean," Carny said, still baffled at the treatment he was getting.

"Food's a whole lot better too," Ike said, going back to his meal.

"Ain't that the truth," Wilson Hadley agreed.

Yes sir. Thanksgiving Day in Twin Rifles was a real eye-opener.

CHAPTER

★ 25 ★

By the time everyone was finished eating, we cleared away the community tables, setting them off to the side of a relatively flat piece of ground. Several of the men got out fiddles and other musical instruments and a dance was soon being partaken in. I never was much at waltzing about on a dance floor, be it inside or out, so when Maria approached me about the subject I politely begged off. That didn't stop her from having a good time though and the next thing I knew she was dancing away in young Riley's arms. It didn't seem to me that she was having any trouble getting over me, none at all.

Of course, dancing wasn't the only reason I wasn't too keen on two-stepping that day. There was that conversation Forrest Haney had with Randall Waite not an hour ago, and that was bothering me something fierce. I'll admit that it wouldn't have surprised me at all to find out that Waite was operating on the shady side of the law, but somehow I didn't think Forrest Haney had gone that far. Or had he? Had he really been in on the bank robbery, some kind of a mastermind even if he hadn't been in on the actual robbing of the bank? If he had indeed conspired to hold up our bank in Twin Rifles, well, he might not have been there in person, but you can bet he was as guilty as the men who'd pulled it off in the first place! Conspiracy, I think Pa had said it was one time. And if that was the truth . . .

I'd kept an eye on Haney after he and Waite had their conversation, another reason I wasn't in the dancing mood. For the most part, he'd stuck around and made social conversation with any number of people at the doings this afternoon. But I could tell he was more than a mite nervous about things, most likely upset over that exchange with his deputy. After all, if what I heard was true, why, Forrest Haney wouldn't be around long enough to retire from his job, much less enjoy life in the town of Sendero. And that was definitely something to worry about.

When he left, I thought he might be going after Randall Waite, so I followed him, keeping a good distance between the two of us. But before I left, I quickly found one of the women and asked her to quick like fix me up a plate with some of the leftover meat for a friend. She hastily filled my order and Forrest Haney was still in sight as I took off after him.

Once inside the city limits, he stayed on the boardwalk in what was basically a deserted town, most of the townsfolk out by the church and attending the dance. If he was tracking Waite he didn't seem to notice or care that the man was nowhere to be seen. When he crossed the street and headed toward his office, I made fast work of ducking into a side alley to make sure he didn't spot me. Once he was inside, I waited a minute before heading for his office. I didn't want to be too obvious about what I'd been doing, following him and all like I had.

"And what do you want?" he asked in a sour disposition when I entered.

I held out the plate of food I'd brought with me. "Didn't see anyone else head back this way with food for your prisoner, so I thought I'd do it," I said with an innocent shrug. "Any harm in that, marshal?"

"I suppose not," he grumbled and got up from his seat and came over to lift up the gingham checkered cloth and see if I had any weapons mixed in among the food.

"Come on, marshal, you don't think I'm that stupid, do you?" I asked.

Forrest Haney raised a cautious eyebrow and, with a frown, said, "You never can tell." Then he let me pass.

"Ah, you're a good man, Wash, a good man," Joshua was saying with a smile once I'd reached his cell. I didn't doubt that he'd likely smelled the food as soon as I'd walked in, for he was right there at the cell door as I passed it through the oblong slot to him. He eagerly began to grab at the chunks of meat, not waiting for a fork, nor caring if he had one or not, I thought.

"How's life treating you?" I said with a smile of my own.

"A whole lot better since you walked through that door," was his reply between mouthfuls of food. "Now if I could get some coffee . . ."

"Marshal?" I said turning to Haney.

"Go ahead, Carston," he grudgingly said with a wave of his hand. Apparently, he didn't want to be bothered with such niceties or manners.

"Sounds like folks hereabouts is having a whaling good time," Joshua said when he'd finished shoveling meat down his gullet. "I could smell the food and hear the music all the way up here," he added, swallowing the last of his coffee and passing cup and plate back through the bars to me.

"I'll bet." I gave a quick glance Haney's way and saw him looking lazily out the window as though dreaming. Maybe he was doing some serious thinking. Then I lowered my own voice and said to Joshua, "Listen, hoss, I'm gonna get you out of this place. Things have been cockeyed ever since I got here."

Joshua snorted like an angry sow I'd seen one time. "Shoot, boy, you ain't telling me nothing I didn't already know a week ago."

"What was that, hill man?" Haney said, suddenly turning about to face us.

"The name's Joshua, not some dadgum label you decided you was gonna throw about me like a rope to a wild mustang." The anger was really coming out in the man now as he spoke in a fiery tone to the lawman.

"I was telling my friend that he's been in your jail far too long," I said, trying to keep a certain amount of control in my own voice, although I'd be the first to admit that I was feeling about as mad as Joshua.

"Oh?" Again the cocked and curious eyebrow.

"Yeah. My friends and me have been doing some asking around the last day or so and we've come up with some real interesting information about you and Richards." I'd let out just a little of what I knew, wanting to see if he'd bite at it like a hungry catfish. Hell, I wasn't about to make a damn fool out of myself if all I'd been gathering was false information. But the only way to find out how true it was seemed to be to ask the man it involved.

Marshal Forrest Haney bit like a hungry catfish.

"Just what is it you're talking about, Carston?" he asked, the curiosity in his voice suddenly gone, replaced by a real healthy dose of caution.

"I'm talking about Richards having two breaks in his leg, enough to keep a normal man all but bedridden. He must have been a real powerful man to have tried breaking jail the way I've heard he did."

"Could be, but you ain't told me everything," Haney said, frowning. "What else is there?"

"Well, according to your undertaker Richards was back shot. Now, maybe you don't have any qualms about shooting a man in the back, Haney, even a man with one hell of a break in his leg, but I know one thing for certain."

"Which is?"

I glanced at Joshua as I said, "My friend ain't nothing close to a back shooter. He's too good a man to do that."

"Thank you, Wash," Joshua said in a humble voice.

"I also heard the conversation you and Randall Waite had in back of the church. You know which one, about how you were the head of this bank robbing gang and just stayed back in the shadows while the others did their work. You remember that, don't you, Haney?" I said with a half smile to let him know I had him cold.

"That's a goddamn lie, Carston, and you know it!" he all but yelled at me from across the room.

"No, it's not, Haney, and I think you know that better than anyone in this town." He didn't like that, small beads of sweat now breaking out on his forehead. I knew I'd made the man uncomfortable at best, maybe even a little scared of the situation he was facing.

"You can't prove nothing, sonny," Forrest Haney said angrily. "Nothing. It'll be Waite's word against mine, you oughtta know that too."

"Could be." I shrugged. "But I think I figured out what happened. It was that bank of ours back in Twin Rifles that Richards and his compadres tried holding up. Pa said more than one of 'em got shot and at least one got away. I'd bet a dollar Richards was the one who got away. I couldn't tell you how he busted that leg of his in two places, but it wouldn't be the first time a man has done something foolish like that on this frontier. The important thing is he headed right back here to see you and let you know how bad off things were for him and the rest.

"Odds are you were talking to him like nothing had ever happened when someone from the town came in, likely that new telegraph operator of yours, with word of the attempted bank robbery. I'd say you pulled a gun on Richards and put him in a cell, making it look like you'd just captured you a bank robber.

"Then, when the two of you were alone, you got to talking and Richards got to demanding an explanation of everything. I don't know what you told him, but I'm thinking he started mouthing off to you about how he was gonna spread the word about you being the head of that bank robbing outfit. And knowing you ain't in the habit of taking sass from anyone, you likely threatened to kill him then and there. Or maybe you told him you'd help him escape, busted leg and all. Then it was just a matter of finding some stranger like Joshua to pin the killing on once you'd back shot him."

"You're smart, kid, but that's nothing more than a story you made up in your head," Haney said. He looked as though he'd regained some of his confidence. "There's still nothing you can prove. Not a thing."

"That may be, Haney, but I've got a notion that if I start making my inquiries more than the mere quiet type, I can likely stir up enough concern over what you *might* have been doing to get a full investigation of you and your deputy started. You wouldn't like that, would you?" I smiled at him, letting him know I hadn't lost any confidence at all over this matter. Oh, I might have been stretching the truth a mite in places, but I was pretty sure I was basically right in what I'd just said.

It would have been interesting to hear what Forrest Haney had to say, but I didn't get the chance to hear, nor did he get the chance to say. A rock came crashing through the window, scattering glass all over the floor and breaking both my and Forrest Haney's concentration.

"What the hell?" he said over his shoulder, only quickly glancing at the mess on the floor.

"Bring him out, lawman! I want him now! Hear me?" At first I couldn't understand the voice, nor identify it, then the back of my memory opened up and I knew it was the drunk I'd first run into at the Avalon Saloon. Turner was his name. The one who'd had a real desire to see Joshua hung. The one I'd wound up in jail over. And now he wanted Joshua.

"Go sleep it off, Turner," Haney yelled out the broken window. "You're drunk. You don't know what you're doing."

I was heading toward the window when a shot rang out from outside and another piece of glass went flying through the air. I ducked, pulling my gun as I did, seeing Haney do the same out of the corner of my eye. From the side of the window I could see Turner and a mob of men who looked as though they had just come from the local armory, each of them carrying some kind of rifle or pistol. I only had a quick look but I'd swear that I saw Randall Waite among the men in that mob.

"Looks like they mean business," I said. "Just what is it you're gonna do, Haney?"

Forrest Haney looked back out at the mob, seeing Randall Waite now just as I had. He pursed his lips in a serious manner, then made what must have been one of the toughest decisions of his life.

"Give me your gun, Carston," he said next, and before I knew it he had his six-gun trained on me. I could have tried to get in my licks but I didn't fancy dying this young, not with a woman like Sarah Ann waiting for me back home.

"What the hell are you doing?" I asked as he took my Colt Conversion model and tossed it on his desk.

"I reckon it's about time I do my own fighting," was all he said as he pushed me back to the cell next to

Joshua's. Once I was inside, he locked it and tossed the keys on his desk, next to my six-gun.

"Now, don't that beat all," Joshua said, flabbergasted as all get out. I couldn't have said it better myself as the two of us watched Forrest Haney, city marshal of Sendero, march out the door to face the mob.

I didn't know for sure, but I had a sneaking suspicion that Forrest Haney had finally found the courage to do his job. And there's something admirable about that.

CHAPTER

★ 26 ★

Come on, Haney, just turn that hillbilly over to us and we'll be done with it," I heard Turner say in a drunken slur. The marshal had left the door to his office open as he'd walked out to face this mob, so I didn't have all that hard a time hearing the conversation.

"Can't do that, Turner, and you know it," Haney said in that gruff manner he could conjure up when he wanted to. I got the distinct impression that he very much wanted to now.

"What the hell are we gonna do, Wash?" Joshua said, a worried look on his face. I knew he didn't like Haney any more than I did, but there is something about seeing one of your own colleagues die that gets you to thinking real hard in a situation like this.

"Damned if I know, hoss," I replied. All I could do was look at my gun and the keys on the marshal's desk and wonder how in the devil I could transfer one or both to me at this moment. I wasn't having an awful lot of luck at it either.

"We gotta do something, Wash, we got to." Joshua seemed awful desperate now and took out that frustration he was feeling by trying to bend apart the bars to his cell. At any other time I would have thought such an act was comical simply because of the impossibility of it, but at the moment I was tempted to try pulling the bars apart my own self. Hell, there didn't seem like a hell of a lot else we could do. And just standing there, why, that was useless as tits on a boar hog.

Maria had the answer to our prayers. I heard the back door fidget and then open as the waitress entered and looked around carefully to see who was in the jail house. In her hand she held a plate full of food, similar, I thought, to the one I had brought Joshua.

"Over here, Maria, over here," Joshua said, a ray of hope in his voice, the thought of food farthest from his mind.

The woman started rushing toward us but I said, "The keys are over on the desk," before she could stop in front of us. She was quick to catch on and had the keys in her hand in no time.

"I was going to bring some food to Joshua," she said as she unlocked our cell doors. "When I saw those men head for the jail too, I knew things were coming to a head so I darted down the alley and waited until I heard the marshal go out the front door."

I checked the loads of the Colt Conversion model as I heard Haney still trying to hold off the mob.

"Who the hell's side are you on anyway, Waite?" I heard the marshal ask after the deputy had made some snide remark about the bunch of them coming up on the boardwalk and taking the marshal apart piece by piece.

"I'm on *my* side, marshal, you should know that by now," the deputy said.

"I reckon there's a lot of things I should know by now," Haney said in what I thought sounded like a voice filled with regret. "Sometimes it just takes a man longer than it should for him to catch on to things." Maybe there was hope for Forrest Haney after all. From the sound of him, he was acting like a stand-up lawman, and there ain't nothing wrong with that, not in my book.

I rummaged through the drawers of the marshal's desk and found what looked like Joshua's gun and gun belt and tossed them to him.

"Thanks, Wash," he said appreciatively. Then, with a sheepish smile, he added, "Don't feel so naked now." To Maria he said, "Begging your pardon, ma'am."

"Of course." Maria smiled.

"Have you got any idea where Riley or Emmett might be?" I asked Maria as I slipped my Colt into its holster. I never did find them, and they were the ones I had been looking for originally.

"I think Emmett said he was going to Martha's to take a nap," she said. "Too much turkey . . . as for Riley, I don't know," she added with a shrug.

"You head back toward the boardinghouse and see if you can round him up," I said, hoping she'd notice the urgency in my voice, for it definitely was real. "Tell him me and Joshua are over at the jail and need a hard-charging cavalryman. I got a notion Haney's gonna need as much help as he can get."

"I'll do my best," she said and was gone, rushing out the back door.

"What say we deal a hand in this game?" I said, asking what one of those big-time writers would call a rhetorical kind of question.

Joshua plunked his hat on his head and loosened the six-gun in his holster. "Wouldn't have it any other way, Wash."

I nodded agreement and we walked out on the boardwalk, taking up stances on either side of Forrest Haney.

There were a good dozen of them standing there facing Haney and they were all well armed. Believe me, it took guts just to walk out on that boardwalk and face these ruffians. Knowing that, Forrest Haney had my respect. Maybe he'd just forgotten what inner courage is for a while. If he had, it seemed to have crawled back inside of him at the right time, for he hadn't cut and run like some men might. No sir. He was standing as tall and straight as a wooden Indian, his granite jaw sticking out as though he were waiting for someone to hang a lantern on it.

"Odds seem a mite agin you, marshal," Joshua said, taking in the same features of this crowd I had.

"It's always nice to have a little backup now and then." The man wasn't about to commend anyone or give them his thanks. Reminded me a bit of Chance.

We'd cut the odds down from the twelve-to-one Forrest Haney had originally been facing to four-to-one. That wasn't the best of odds, mind you, but at least when we died these fellows would know who they had been tangling with. I'll guarantee you that, mister!

"Odds are getting slimmer, boys," Haney called out then, as cool as a cucumber. "You sure you don't want to call this shindig off? Might be more than a couple of you wind up visiting boot hill on a permanent basis if you don't." I didn't have to look into his eyes to know he meant every word he said, and I had a notion most of the men in this crowd knew that too.

"And the man you yahoos is a-wanting is standing right here, so if you're feeling right froggy, why, you go ahead and jump 'cause I'm in the mood for catching bullfrogs today," Joshua said in a nasty tone.

No one said anything in reply except Randall Waite, and he seemed to be ignoring Joshua and his threat. Of course, a lot of these men were looking back and forth among themselves with questioning looks in their eyes. Waite must have figured he was going to lose his mob so he gave them another bone to chew on.

"In case you men didn't know it, Forrest Haney is the man behind this bank robbing gang," he said, his voice filled with hatred.

"What?" a number of shocked voices said in unison.

"Is that true, marshal?" another man asked.

"It's a downright lie, Harry, and you know it," was the lawman's bitter reply. He almost sounded as convincing with this crowd as he had with me when I asked the same question not long ago in the jail house.

Before anything else could be said, I heard the voice of young Riley as he appeared on the boardwalk and took up a stance next to Joshua on the far side of our group.

"Odds don't look so good, marshal," he said, then went into a minor coughing fit. Once he was through he spit out another huge gob of spit, which landed on a boot of one of Randall Waite's tough-looking *amigos.* I could tell by the look on his face that the man didn't like it at all.

"Odds are getting better all the time," Haney said, sticking to his unemotional tone of voice.

"You'd think this was a gamblers' reunion, as much as people are talking odds around here," Joshua said.

"What about those charges Deputy Waite is making?" Harry, one of the lynch mob, asked again.

"I told you once it's a goddamn lie. I ain't about to tell you again." Forrest Haney wasn't going to put up with much more of this.

"Say, what the hell's going on here?" I heard Emmett say from down the street. Out of the corner of my eye I caught sight of him pulling his suspenders up and over his shoulders as he walked toward us, his battered cavalryman's hat sitting at a cocky angle atop his head. "Young lady comes up to my room and wakes me up in the middle of my nap, says the town's gone to hell in a hand basket." Emmett had what you'd likely call a booming voice anyway, so by the time he reached us and his words were out, why, there was no doubt that everyone in the vicinity had heard him.

He took up a position next to me.

"Seems to be some concern about whether or not we're breaking up a lynch mob or trying to hold a kangaroo court here in the city streets," I said.

"Do tell."

"And I'm the one they're a-wanting to lynch, if you can believe it," Joshua said emphatically.

191

"You!" Emmett sounded purely flabbergasted at Joshua's words. "Oh, no, don't you worry none, Joshua, ain't no one gonna hang you while I'm around. No, sir."

Randall Waite broke out in laughter. "You don't seriously think some potbellied old fart like you is gonna keep me from hanging a man in this town?"

"If it's my friend, yes," Emmett growled.

"Let me tell you something, Waite," I said in an even voice. "On his worst day, this potbellied old fart, as you call him, could take you apart and feed you to the wolves with no effort at all."

"Damn sure betcha," Emmett added with a wink and a nod.

"I've had enough of this swill," Turner said in his drunken garble. He didn't know how true he had spoken, for when he began pulling his pistol, he'd opened the ball.

"That's it, boys. Boots and saddles!" Emmett yelled. "Boots and saddles!" By the time he was finished speaking, he too had his six-gun coming out of his cross-draw holster. That was Emmett for you, never put off until tomorrow what you can get taken care of today. Breaking horses, working a farm, or killing a man, it didn't make a lick to Emmett.

Turner's pistol was the first to go off, his shot striking Emmett high in the shoulder. But like I say, Emmett was a tough old bull, and even as he was reeling back toward the front of the jail he managed to get a shot off at Turner. His bullet hit the man square in the chest and Turner slumped to the ground, a pool of blood forming on his shirt front.

Forrest Haney and I both had our guns out at the same time, firing at Randall Waite in front of us. As far as I know, we both hit our mark, but Waite got off a couple of shots before he went down. One of them took Haney in the chest and he fell back against the wall, still holding his six-gun. Then something whistled past me and I thought it was a bullet tugging at my shirtsleeve and paid little attention to it. All I knew was that the Colt Conversion model Chance had bragged so much to me about had felt awful comfortable in my hand as it went to work, just as it was supposed to.

By the time I saw Randall Waite raising his pistol for one last try at us, he was already down on his knees, a look of pain on his face. I was cocking that Colt to do him in when Joshua beat me to it and put two slugs of his own into the deputy, finishing his life here on earth. He was dead by the time he toppled over, face first in the dirt.

But the biggest and loudest surprise of them all came from young Riley. I reckon I heard his shots most distinctly because there were so many of them. Yet, I didn't think I could count them all. What I saw was three men falling dead in the street before him, all three on the left side of where Randall Waite had stood. And they had all died at the hands of the young man I knew only as Riley. The last thing I saw Riley do was holster his six-gun, cough a mite, and spit on one of the bodies. Then he looked down at Forrest Haney.

"You picked a bad choice of friends, *amigo,* a bad choice," he said, shaking his head.

We seemed to have the rest of this crowd rattled for they appeared fearful in their desire to carry this fight on any further.

Martha Stoner settled the whole matter for, like

always, she had a handle on things. This time it was a double-barreled shotgun. The blast went off across the street and scared the hell out of all of us.

"Stop it, you damn fools!" she yelled and visibly cocked the second barrel for all to see. "This is supposed to be a day of peace, not war. Now, go home, all of you. Get the doctor. For godsake clean up this mess you've made or this second load will go right into all of you." Just like Forrest Haney had meant every threatening word he'd spoken, so did Martha Stoner, and I think we all knew it. One glance at the long barrel was enough to make believers out of all of us.

Joshua and Emmett were best of friends, so it didn't surprise me to see Joshua run past me to Emmett, who was still standing even though he'd been shot and was bleeding some. Me, I kneeled down beside Forrest Haney, who had wound up in a sitting position against the front of his jail. It seemed strange that he was coughing, almost as badly as Riley, but this wasn't spit dribbling out of his mouth now. No, it was blood and that was a sure sign of bleeding inside a man.

"You can let go of that pistol now, marshal," I said, noting that Haney still had an iron grip on his six-gun. "The fighting's over for the day."

But the man seemed to have other things on his mind. Maybe he knew he was dying and needed to say something. That was usually the way of it with a man, especially at the last. Of course, I knew when I saw the spreading pool of blood on his chest that he didn't have long left.

"You take me in to your Twin Rifles and you'll have the whole of your gang of bank robbers, son," he said through bubbles of blood at the corner of his mouth.

"Then it was you."

He nodded, emitting what I thought to be a sigh of relief. I reckon it was as close as he'd gotten to feeling an easing of the burden he was carrying for quite some time.

"Me and Richards and the rest you've got in your town," he admitted. Then he bit his lip, a look of thought crossing his face in the last few minutes he had left, and he said, "Thanks, Carston, I appreciate your help. And the words, I appreciate the words." Forrest Haney had finally let down his guard and said thanks.

Then his head slumped forward and he was dead.

In a way it was ironic. I'd started out trying to prove that Forrest Haney had something to do with the evil that was going on in Sendero, and in my own clumsy way I'd done just that—proven him to be the villain I was looking for. Or at least one of them. But in the end I'd wound up fighting beside the man, holding a good deal of respect for him at the very end. It was strange how things happened in life.

I looked about and saw Emmett and Joshua, but not Riley. The crowd that was once a mob had taken Martha Stoner's advice and dispersed, no longer in sight.

Maria was suddenly at my side, inspecting my arm.

"You're hurt," she said. "Sit down and I'll take care of you."

"Well, be quick about it," I replied, still looking about the town of Sendero, seeing Riley nowhere in sight. "I need to find that kid, Riley."

"He's gone," she said. "When the shooting stopped, he rode out of town."

CHAPTER

★ 27 ★

Hearing that Riley had ridden out of town after our gunfight was over was a bit of a surprise to me. As much as the young man had spouted off about hitting what he aimed for and all, it didn't seem like him to all of a sudden get humble about his accomplishments and ride out of town without notice. Still, if nothing else I wanted to catch up with Riley and tell him how grateful I was to him for helping us out when we were between a rock and a hard place. Maybe Forrest Haney couldn't find it in him to say thank you to a man when it was called for, but I could. I wanted to shake Riley's hand and give him a slap on the back for a job well done. And if that meant trailing the man out of town to find him, then I'd do it.

Emmett was in the process of being patched up by Maria and Martha when I saddled my mount at the livery and tried picking up any trail Riley might have left as he departed Sendero. And I'll tell you, it wasn't much. Even with the sun out that afternoon, I had a devil of a time picking up his trail but I finally managed to do so. Once I had it, though, it wasn't all that hard to follow.

I might not have caught it at all if it hadn't been for the little drops of blood I spotted about a mile out of town, the ones that fell next to the prints of his horse's hooves. I knew he couldn't go far then, knew he would have to find someplace to rest up and do it soon.

He did. His trail led me to a small rocky area not far from a grove of cottonwoods a few miles out of town.

"You don't want to come no farther, friend," I heard him yell at me as I neared his position. I couldn't mistake Riley's voice and that raspy cough of his that followed it.

"Shooting's over, Riley. I didn't come to harm you, you should know that," I said in as peaceful a manner as I could.

"Well, I *don't* want to see you, lawman," he said forcefully. Sounded downright serious about it, he did.

"How come?" I asked and slowly walked toward his voice, determined one way or another to see what kind of wild hair had crawled up inside this man.

"Don't, Wash. It ain't pretty, believe me."

We were both silent for a few minutes then, the only silence being the afternoon breeze picking up and whispering through the rocks. Riley sat there and gasped and choked and spit all that time, not saying another word. Me, I worked my way around the back of the rocks I figured him to be hiding behind and took one big step out toward him.

Riley was right. It wasn't a pretty sight at all. His whole side was bloodied up, a small river of the red stuff flowing down the side of his pants leg. It had to be a wound that was getting more and more serious as time went by.

"What the hell happened to you?" I asked in surprise as I took in the sight of him.

"Reckon I ain't the only one who hits what he aims at, huh?"

"It would seem." By then I had conjured up enough worry about the man and his condition so I didn't stop to hear what he might have to say about staying away from him. He'd been hurt and hurt badly and he needed attention, medical attention, and needed it now. "Don't be foolish," I added when his hand dropped down to his six-gun as though he were going to draw it again.

"Just leave me alone, Wash," he said after coughing and spitting up a mouthful of blood. "Don't embarrass me by taking me back to town to have some fancy doctor take a look at me. You and I both know I'm done for, so leave me alone. Besides, a man ought to be able to choose his dying place."

"Now you're talking stupid, Riley, plain stupid," I said in reply, even though I knew the truth of the words he spoke. The man had been hit and was bleeding on his insides as well as his outsides, and that wasn't any good.

"I come into this world alone, Wash, and I'd just as soon leave it that way, so do me a favor and ride on back to town and leave me be," he said, once again spitting out huge gobs of bloody spit.

There was too much I wanted to say at that moment and all the words got stuck in my throat as I tried to get them out. I glanced over toward a cottonwood, thinking maybe the words'd come to me if I gave them a minute.

"I can't leave you alone, Riley," I said as I turned to the wounded young man, only to see that his eyes were closed and his head had slumped to the side, as though he were asleep. "I just can't."

Neither of us had an awful lot to say about the situation then. Riley was dead and that was that.

I got more than my share of stares as I rode back into Sendero, leading Riley's horse with the dead man lying across its saddle. I stared back just as hard as those who stared. I didn't stop until I'd reached the undertaker's office and found someone to handle Riley's body and give him a decent burial. When I was through, I headed back to Martha Stoner's boarding-house to see how Emmett was doing.

"Oh, he'll be fine," Martha said after I inquired about my friend. "Didn't get hit as bad as everyone thought he did." She smiled and poured me some coffee, reassuring me again that Emmett would be fit to ride in a day or two. "You, on the other hand, look like you've lost a good friend." Which was when I told her about Riley and how he had died. I had an idea Martha had liked the boy as much as I did.

I was silent for a while as I drank my coffee, mulling over the thoughts of what had happened today. That feeling I'd had this morning about this day turning out to be a bad one had come true. Oh, there might have been a lot of people who had enjoyed a day of Thanksgiving, but there were also a handful of them who had died before the sun set. And death was not a subject I cared to think on all that much.

"Oh, there you are," I heard Maria say as she entered the boardinghouse and spotted me having coffee with Martha. "I thought I saw you come in here."

"I hope you haven't got some crazy idea, Maria," I said adamantly, "for I'm really not in the mood for it."

"No, nothing like that," she went on, smiling. Silence seemed to be the order of the day about then, for she stood there in her own calm mood before speaking to me again. "I've done some thinking on what you told me this afternoon . . . and I guess I was wrong all along."

"Excuse me, children," Martha said, suddenly looking as awkward as she sounded, "but I've got things to do in the kitchen." With that she departed, leaving Maria and me to ourselves.

"You really love that Sarah Ann, don't you?" she asked.

"As a matter of fact I do. Why do you ask?"

"There was a young man who passed through here during the war years. He took a liking to me and almost started talking marriage." She reached inside a pocket to her dress and pulled out a mighty fancy looking ring. "Even gave me this." She held the ring out for my inspection. "Then one day he disappeared. Never did see him again."

"Nice ring."

She blushed as she said, "Why don't you give it to your wife? I think she'd like it."

Then she placed the ring firmly in my hand, kissed me lightly on the cheek, and was gone as quick as she'd come.

CHAPTER
★ 28 ★

The Reverend Appleby made it a point to stay for another day so the town could bury the casualties of that gunfight good and proper. I reckon it was the Christian feeling that had come out in most of them that Thanksgiving Day that sparked the idea.

Emmett was looking mighty peaked, but he and I made it to the funeral, more for the sake of Riley than any of the others. From what I'd come to know of the lad, he seemed like a lonely man born to a lonely, tough world. It just seemed right that he have someone there to say good-bye to him at the end. I didn't pay much attention to the flowery words the preacher was speaking, for all I had running through my mind was the pitiful way Riley had died after acting in such a heroic manner.

"I wonder if anyone in Sendero will remember what he did?" Emmett asked after the services.

"I wouldn't count on it," I said as we headed back to the boardinghouse.

"I will," Maria said behind us. Apparently, she had been close enough to hear our conversation.

"Oh?" Emmett said with cocked eye.

"In his own way he was a nice young man," she said. "Sort of reminded me of that fellow I told you about yesterday," she added, speaking to me in particular.

I said I knew, although Emmett seemed totally confused about the whole conversation. When he didn't ask for further details, I didn't volunteer them. Some things are better left unsaid.

Emmett spent most of that day sleeping while Joshua did close to the same, but doing it in a bed that was nothing like those lumpy cots in the city jail. I reckon it was his way of celebrating Thanksgiving, even if it was a day late.

At Emmett's insistence, we left the next day. Hell, the man was out in back of Martha Stoner's kitchen, swinging an axe with one arm and doing a halfway successful job of chopping deadwood into sizes small enough to fit Martha's Dutch oven. Naturally, it was all in trade for a couple of extra slices of meat on the breakfast plate.

Once we were saddled and ready to ride, we stopped by Martha's to say good-bye and were each given enough meat and biscuits to feed us for three days on the trail.

"You boys watch your topknot, you hear?" she said out front of her boardinghouse. The three of us tipped our hats and said a profuse amount of thank-yous to the woman before riding at a lope out of Sendero. I thought I saw Maria inside Annie's Place as we rode by it, watching us ride off. Maybe I was seeing things but I also thought I saw her raise a hand to wave to us—or was it me?—as we left. But I had a notion it was only a halfhearted gesture for the woman had one of the saddest looks on her face that I had ever seen.

If it hadn't been for the sun staying out as long as it did that day, we would have frozen our tails off by sunset, of that I am certain. Not that it was all that warm, you understand, but the sun helped bring some extra warmth through our jackets, and as cold as it had been on my way to Sendero I didn't think I'd ever be able to recover from it. The only thing I could recall keeping my mind off of the cold had been that tooth of mine that had gone bad on the way to Sendero. Today the sun had helped some. Some good hot coffee at our noon camp spread some of the warmth too.

Emmett shivered as the three of us squatted around a small fire at noon. Maybe he was a mite feverish. It wouldn't be the first time a man had gotten that way from a bullet wound. I had intentionally kept the pace of our riding down to a fast lope because of Emmett's condition. As enthusiastic as he'd seemed that morning, I had noticed he again looked a bit on the peaked side by midmorning. And he hadn't complained when I'd slowed the pace even more, so I knew he wasn't in the best of shape, gunshot wound or no gunshot wound. I let it pass for the moment, knowing Emmett was a full-grown man and didn't want to be babied or anything, particularly by another man.

We rode steady the rest of the day. It was nothing a Pony Express rider would want to brag about but we were heading back to Twin Rifles and all the danger in our lives had passed as far as we were concerned. So riding nice and easy was the order of the day for us, even if it was unspoken. But it was during the evening meal that I got curious.

Emmett took to shivering again, even after what I thought was a decent meal for being on the trail. I glanced at Joshua to see if he had noticed this turn in Emmett. A silent raise of the eyebrows told me he had.

"Feeling kind of feverish, are you, Emmett?" Joshua finally asked.

"Yeah. I noticed you were doing some of that shivering at noon camp," I said. "We can always lay over a mite tomorrow and see if you shake it if it comes to it."

"Nope, ain't a fever at all," was Emmett's reply. "One thing I always got lucky at, I reckon. Never did fever from a gunshot wound." I leaned forward and removed a glove, placing the back of my hand on the ex-cavalryman's forehead.

"By God, he's right, Joshua," I said in surprise.

"Well, then what is it, man?" Joshua said with a good deal of concern. "Just what all's a-bothering you to cause you shivers and shakes and such?"

Emmett sipped some of his coffee and thought a bit about what to say. Finally, he looked at me and said, "You remember that Llano Estacado we come back across with Uncle Charlie Goodnight a year back?"

"Sure." Chance and I had been in a bind for money one spring back and had broken a good number of mustangs and sold them to Charlie Goodnight, who also had us along on his first trail drive. We'd headed west, across the Staked Plains, covering some six hundred miles before reaching our destination. That trail we'd blazed was now called the Goodnight-Loving Trail and headed west to the New Mexican Territory and up into the Colorado Territory. Emmett had come along as a wrangler, being good with horses like he was. "What about it?"

"Remember how we come back with Uncle Charlie's twelve thousand dollars and toward the end I kept telling you boys I had a notion someone was trailing us?"

"Yeah," I said with a nod. It had taken us close to seven days to recross the Staked Plains and get back to Fort Belknap, where we'd originated the herd of two thousand cattle. I nodded again and added, "Did some shivering back then too, as I recall. Wondered if you wasn't feverish then too."

"Uh-huh. And Uncle Charlie said not to worry about it, it would pass."

"Yeah, but you said it wasn't a fever then either, as I recall," I said.

"Well, just what did you say, dad blame you!" Joshua all but exploded. I reckon me and Emmett remembering the incident had been like some wild story that had gotten Joshua's interest, for he hadn't been there.

"What he said was he felt like the Comanches had followed us and was tracking us down," I said.

"And were they?" Joshua asked excitedly.

"Nope, wasn't Comanch' at all," Emmett said with a slight smile.

"Turned out it was a handful of ruffians who tried to steal Uncle Charlie's herd once upon a time," I said. They had talked big and acted tough. The trouble was they couldn't match their words with their actions. And tough as they might have thought they were, most of them had wound up dead when they'd tried to steal Uncle Charlie's twelve thousand dollars from the sale of his cattle.

Emmett set the cup of coffee down and shivered again. Then he reached up behind his neck and rubbed it some, as though to massage his muscles. A worried look came to his face and he said, "I hate to say it, boys, but I'm having that same feeling now. Had it all day, ever since we left Sendero."

Neither Joshua nor I said a word. We just looked at one another in puzzled silence. Emmett had to be mistaken, was all I could think. He had to be. Hell, we'd left all of our problems in Sendero and most of them were dead. All any of us wanted now was to get back to the quiet life of Twin Rifles. Still, I found that as the night wore on, one nagging question stuck in my mind.

Who in the hell could possibly be tracking us? And why?

CHAPTER
★ 29 ★

You sure this is where Waite said that deputy lived, Wade?" Jethro Frazier said to his cousin.

Wade Frazier, the older of the Frazier Cousins, squinted at the sign that read TWIN RIFLES and nodded to Jethro. "Yup, this is where he said it was. Twin Rifles. Yeah, that's it."

"I don't care what town it is," the third rider, another Frazier named Hanson said. "I say we find us a place that serves up a decent meal and get us some of it."

All three of the Frazier Cousins appeared just as wild and rowdy as they had in Sendero when Marshal Forrest Haney had put them in jail for the fight they'd started with Emmett in Annie's Place. Each wore a scraggly looking beard. And when they smiled, which was seldom, there was usually a tooth or two missing from their mouth. Their clothes were secondhand at best, torn and frayed at the elbows and knees, probably a disgrace to any citizen of Sendero or Twin Rifles where civilized people claimed to live. But the Fraziers didn't seem to care one whit what anyone else might have thought of them. Such vanity seemed far from their minds, although some would likely dispute just what it was these cousins had between their ears.

At one time there had been four Fraziers, but Harrison was dead now, which was why these three cousins had come to Twin Rifles. The four cousins had originally been hired by Randall Waite for the sharp-shooting of Wash Carston and that young upstart Riley. They had attempted to do just that when the two men had been out hunting turkeys late one morning. But trouble had developed when they had missed their mark and Harrison had taken a couple of slugs in his back as the four men tried to escape before being killed as well. Waite wasn't happy about their failed attempt at killing Wash Carston and his friend, but he had been thinking all the while. Waite desperately wanted Carston dead and had instructed the Fraziers that if he shouldn't succeed in killing the deputy U.S. marshal while he was in Sendero, the three cousins should track the man down to Twin Rifles, where Carston claimed to make his home. Each of the cousins had received fifty dollars with the promise of fifty more should they be successful in killing Carston this time. Now, the Fraziers were just as greedy as the next man for money, but this trip had been more for the revenge in having lost a cousin than any kind of assassination. Either way they had the killing of Wash Carston on their mind.

They rode into Twin Rifles, paying little attention to the stares they drew from the townspeople, for they had long ago learned to ignore them. They pulled their horses to a halt in front of the Porter Cafe and barged in as though they owned the place.

Sarah Ann seated them and made sure to keep her distance, noting that none of them smelled any too clean. At first glance, all she could say for them was that they were reasonably well mannered. She took their order, poured them coffee, and disappeared into the kitchen.

"Say, ma'am, would you know where I could find a feller by the name of Wash Carston?" Wade Frazier asked her when she brought their meals a short time later.

The question shook her, for Sarah Ann could remember a similar such request of a gruff-looking man who had come asking for Wash's brother, Chance. The man hadn't turned out to be a friend at all, but a man intent on killing Chance. The trouble had been he'd wound up trying to go through Wash first, and at that time Wash had seen better days.

"Why, yes, as a matter of fact, I do," she replied to the man's question. "I believe he has a ranch outside of town. Runs it with his brother from what I hear." She was about to turn away when she stopped and asked, "Do you have business with him, if I may ask?"

Wade Frazier shrugged and tried to look as innocent as possible, a feat hard to accomplish for the man. "Nothing, really. A mutual friend of ours recommended we stop by and see old Wash. Just a friendly visit."

"I see," Sarah Ann said and was gone. In the kitchen, she looked at Big John and said, "Papa, I don't like those men."

Big John Porter slowly pulled back the curtain to a portion of the kitchen area that enabled him to see any amount of customers who were seated in his cafe, saw the Fraziers and shook his head.

"Darlin'," he said. "Ugly as they are, I doubt that their own mothers could have liked any one of that crew."

We rode into Twin Rifles a little after noon, I gauged, if my sense of the sun was anywhere close to accurate. The first thing I wanted to do was rush over to the Porter Cafe and see Sarah Ann, but decided against it and instead headed for Pa's office.

"Well, as I live and breathe," Pa said as he came to the door of his office and took in what I imagine he thought to be a sight for sore eyes. "The three of you pilgrims actually did come back!"

"Why, shore, Will, what'd you think we was doing, fixing to take off and spend the season hunting?" Joshua said and stuck out a paw for his boss.

"You know, I was fixing to saddle up and come after you fellas my own self tomorrow," Pa said as he took his deputy's hand in his own and gave it a good pump.

"None the worse for wear either," I said.

"Except for you." Pa took in Emmett's bandaged chest and added, "Now, what in the devil happened to you boys, anyway?"

"These two can tell you, Pa," I said, my anxiousness

211

to see my wife overwhelming me. "I've got to go see Sarah Ann."

"Then what are you waiting around here for?" Pa said and shooed me off before leading Emmett and Joshua into his office and what I was sure was a cup of coffee to prime their whistles so they'd tell our story.

I entered the Porter Cafe, my eyes looking for no one but Sarah Ann. When I saw her, she was coming back from a table in the rear. She tossed her order book down on a table and rushed into my arms. Me, I kissed her right then and there. Long and hard. Intimacy may be for private times, but to tell the truth I didn't care who was watching at that moment.

"You don't know how glad I am to see you," she blurted out once our lips had parted. "So much has happened, there's so much to tell."

"I know how you feel," I replied. I paused a moment, considered the question and asked, "Did those Hadleys give you any more trouble?"

"Well," she started and followed it with, "actually no. You wouldn't believe what's happened. Honest, Wash!"

She showed me a seat in the middle of the dining room, poured me coffee, and left without even taking my order. She knew that once I'd been on the trail for any length of time I could eat almost anything, as long as it was hot and well done, so I'd likely wind up with a steak and potatoes.

There were a few customers still seated at their tables and enjoying their meals. Me, I was so thrilled at the sight of Sarah Ann that I couldn't have cared less who they were or what they were doing. All I knew was I couldn't wait for Sarah Ann to get off work and take her home and talk to her—among other things.

Sarah Ann had brought me my plate of food and I'd just started to eat when I heard her give out a short yell.

"Let go of me, I said!" she said in a loud voice. When I looked up, I saw three men sitting at a table near the front door to the cafe. One of them had an iron grip on Sarah Ann's arm and was holding her still. "Wash, help me!"

In an instant I had pushed myself away from the table and was on my way to Sarah Ann's side, unaware of what else may have been going on around me.

"You heard her, mister," I said without even looking at the man that well.

"I thought that would get you here, Carston," the man said with a leer as he let go of my wife's arm. It was then I realized that he was one of those crazy Frazier Cousins I'd had a run-in with at Sendero.

He no sooner let go of Sarah Ann than he took a swing at me, landing a hard right on my jaw and knocking me back onto a table top. I rolled off the table, slightly dazed as I fell to the floor. And then everything got confused.

"I should have known you'd wind up like that, Wash," I heard another familiar voice say to me. When I looked up I saw Carny Hadley pass me by. Jesus, Mary, and Joseph! Now the Hadley Brothers were going after Sarah Ann too!

Except they weren't. I think. Carny Hadley brought one of his big fists down on the man who'd been holding Sarah Ann in his grip, knocking him back against the wall with a big, hard blow. Then Wilson and Ike Hadley were there too, doing basically the same thing to the other two Frazier Cousins.

By the time I was on my feet, Big John had opened

the door to his establishment and was standing aside as the Hadley Brothers pushed the Fraziers out the door, one by one. I'll tell you, hoss, I couldn't believe my eyes!

I followed the lot of them outside on the boardwalk, only to see Carny, Wilson, and Ike Hadley beat the living bejesus out of all three of the Fraziers.

Mind you now, I only had one really good arm, having been shot my own self over at Sendero, but I made good use of it.

One of the Fraziers used an Indian kick on Ike Hadley, quickly bringing him to the ground. Although the man was on his back, he was determined to kill his opponent, one way or the other. He began pulling his own six-gun out, likely wanting to shoot Ike, which is where I stepped in.

That Colt Conversion came out of my holster like some piece of lightning, slick as grease, I tell you. It only took a second for me to have it out and pointing dead center at the Frazier on the ground.

"You cock that gun, mister, and the liveliest thing about you is gonna be your shaking body as it dies right where you lie," I growled. He didn't have to hear it twice to know that I meant business. But then looking down the business end of a pistol will usually do that to a man.

Carny and Wilson Hadley were holding their own against the two other Fraziers. Watching them, I still couldn't believe my eyes. The Hadleys were actually fighting with me and not against me!

"Isn't it something?" Sarah Ann said at my side, as she too watched the men who I was sure she used to fear.

"I'll say."

"Like I said, there's a lot to tell, especially about those Hadley boys."

"All right, what in the devil are you boys doing now?" Pa said as he entered the foray. But he wasn't talking to the Fraziers, he was addressing himself to the Hadley Brothers. "Come on, Carny, let the poor man be," he continued, pulling Carny Hadley off of one of the Fraziers. "It looks like you've almost killed the man as it is."

Carny jerked his arm away from Pa's grip, the meanness coming out in him now. "Hell, I'm on your side!"

"What are you talking about, boy?" Pa asked, a confused look on his face.

But it was Sarah Ann who stepped forward to clarify everything. "I'm afraid he's right, Papa Will," she said in her usual soft voice. "That man had me in his grip and Carny, Wilson, and Ike came to my defense. And that's a fact."

"Is that right?" Pa asked me.

"I'd say so."

"In that case," he said, addressing the Hadley Brothers now, "stop beating these sorry asses and put 'em on their raggedy horses and let's take 'em to the city limits. Now that you've beat the hell out of them, I reckon they'll be calm enough to listen to me speechify what ain't allowed in Twin Rifles."

And the Hadley Brothers did just that.

And so did Pa.

CHAPTER

★ 30 ★

The Fraziers never did come back to Twin Rifles that I know of, at least not after Pa got through reading to them from the book. I do believe he even showed them a few pictures too.

Sarah Ann spent the better part of a week telling me how much the Hadley Brothers had changed, how they'd showed up at church on Thanksgiving Day and even volunteered to help her keep peace if there was ever any trouble in the Porter Cafe again. That day I'd gotten back they had been eating a meal there and found a way to show their good faith when that Frazier had grabbed Sarah Ann by the arm. If anything, the Hadleys were opportunists. That much I knew had not changed.

But before I let Sarah Ann do all that explaining, I got Big John to let her off early for the day and I took her home. Chance wasn't around, probably still out hunting wild mustangs if my guess was right.

Once the horses were put up, I went back in the house and held Sarah Ann close to me, kissing her. Then I reached in my pocket and pulled out the ring that Maria had given me. I do believe she almost fainted the way she looked at it.

"Oh, Wash, it's beautiful." She sighed. Like any woman, she spent a minute or so admiring the ring in the light and the different ways it shone on the ring.

"But not as beautiful as you," I said and lifted her face up to mine and kissed her again.

"Oh, Wash, I love you so," she said and hugged me as hard as she could.

"I know, honey, I know." I knew then that I could never fall for another woman, not as long as I had my Sarah Ann.

That must have been when it hit her. After all, here was her near-poor husband handing her a ring that had a lot more than sparkle to it. Her eyes got curious and she raised an eyebrow to me. "Now, just where would *you* get a piece of jewelry like *this?*" she asked in a stern manner.

Now, hoss, you know good and well I wasn't about to tell my wife about Maria! Not if I wanted to keep the woman I had in my arms . . . well, in my arms. So I used what Pa would call the direct approach.

"Sarah Ann," I said, looking down into her loving eyes.

"Yes, Wash," she replied with a sigh.

"Don't ask stupid questions." Then, before she could think of anything to respond with, I kissed her like I meant it, something that wasn't hard to do at all.

Printed in the United States
By Bookmasters